Strong - A Fairy Tale Retelling of the Princess and the Pea

The Crown and the Sceptre, Volume 2

Kristina J Jordan

Published by Kristina J Jordan, 2021.

STRONG - A FAIRY TALE RETELLING OF THE PRINCESS AND THE PEA

First edition. July 10, 2021.

Copyright © 2021 Kristina J Jordan.

ISBN: 979-8201587581

Written by Kristina J Jordan.

Also by Kristina J Jordan

The Crown and the Sceptre
Free A Fairy Tale Retelling of Rapunzel
Strong - A Fairy Tale Retelling of the Princess and the Pea
True A Fairy Tale Retelling of Puss in Boots
Pretty - A fairy Tale Retelling of the Frog Prince
Loyal - A Fairy Tale Retelling of Red Riding Hood

PROLOGUE

Celine adjusted her rustling skirt and gazed at the flock of seagulls swooping and diving out the window, jealous of their freedom. One week ago—one very long week ago—she had pranced in the castle gates, leading the first Lovanian delegation to the newly released kingdom of Iasia. Unfortunately for Celine, who loved adventure and hated sitting still, that was the last bit of action she was likely to see for a while.

"And, wouldn't you agree, your Highness?"

Celine jerked her attention from the window at the gentle voice.

"Oh, yes, definitely. That would be fantastic." Celine pasted on her court smile, pointing it at Queen Abigail. Queen Abigail—only recently thrust into the royal role when Queen Penelope had come to a traitorous and unbecoming end— was desperate to make up for the shortcomings of her predecessor queen.

"Wonderful!" A practiced smile graced Queen Abigail's face. Celine's finger twitched as she focused on the embroidery in her lap. Hopefully, she hadn't just agreed to anything too outrageous. Although, with Queen Abigail, that was highly unlikely. She shot a considered look at the Queen's elegant gown and prim hair.

"We must arrange a time for you two to meet then. It's *such* a shame he went on a hunting trip just when you arrived. Men can be so inconsiderate, don't you think?" Queen Abigail bestowed another smile on Celine—this one held a disapproving air aimed toward the members of the hunting trip. "He should be back before the end of next week, though. I'm sure he'll be so delighted. He told me he only wanted to marry a *real* princess."

Celine's eyes slid toward Abigail, her polite expression slipping. "Did he?" She kept her voice placid and calm, but her mind...her mind raced. If only she paid attention, she wouldn't have agreed to whatever ridiculous notion Queen Abigail had come up with. She pinched her fingers together tightly, a bundle of nerves clenching in her chest.

"Obviously, we'll wait to make the official agreement after the two of you meet. We aren't so archaic that we would fob you off on each other sight unseen. But this is such a relief. You just don't know how hard it was when our family was thrown into the royal role so suddenly. To have an alliance, especially with Lovan, would make such a difference."

"Certainly," Celine choked out, hoping her voice was airy. Despite the mild temperature, sweat stuck the stiff folds of her dress to her clammy skin. Mother and Father would be so disappointed in her if she spoiled her very first delegation; she needed to find a way out of this mess. And quickly, because judging by the glint in Queen Abigail's eye, plans were being hatched—plans Celine intended to have nothing to do with. She came here for an adventure, not to be roped into a marriage with a prince she had never even laid eyes on before. To buy time, she added a spoonful of honey to her tea as she balanced the delicate China cup in her hand.

"Oh yes, I will have to consult my mother and father in person, of course." A serene smile sat on her lips. There, that should stall things until she could fix the situation. She took a sip and let the sweetness sit on her tongue for a moment before reaching for a meringue, choosing one with a dusting of toasted coconut flakes.

"Of course, my dear." Queen Abigail's eyes darted to the side.

"And, long engagements are traditional for Lovanians. Especially royalty."

"Really?" Queen Abigail furrowed her brow. "Didn't your brother get married after just a few months?"

"Um... yes. But those were very special circumstances. They had to get permission from the king."

"Ah, well then, that shouldn't be a problem for you, my dear. After all, he is your father." Queen Abigail busied herself choosing a strand of thread for her embroidery.

Celine bit her lip and watched the clock, willing the minutes to tick by until she could go find a place to think. There must be some way, some polite way, to preserve relations between Lovan and Iasia but tell Queen Abigail that she didn't want to marry her son.

THE NEXT MORNING, CELINE slipped down to the arena early. It felt good to stretch her muscles. She whirled, twirling her sword around her head before she tossed it to her other hand and struck.

"That's a new move." Lord Gunther panted as he dove out of range of the shining weapon.

"I know. I saw it at the exhibition they had the other day, and I wanted to try it." Celine executed a series of feints before flicking her sword to the left, catching Gunther off guard.

"You were good; but now you're getting better than ever." Gunther rubbed his wrist and picked up his sword, shaking off the dust of the arena. If these weren't practice swords, you would have unmanned me. You used to never get that close."

"I've been practicing." Celine beamed at the compliment. After the last few days of attending parties full of strangers, drinking tea, and attending too many events to count, it felt good to move. "Although I'm going to get rusty if I stay here much longer. I haven't had a minute."

"I know, but it's just another two weeks."

"But Gunther, I don't think I'm very good at these diplomatic trips." Celine sat down on the wooden railing at the side of the arena.

"I made the biggest mistake today; Father is going to kill me when he finds out, especially after I pressured him into letting me come."

"What mistake?" Gunther's eyes held a wary expression. "The only time I left you was when you went to have tea with Abigail."

"That's exactly when it happened. At the tea, it was just so *boring*, I got distracted. And I think—I think I agreed to something, and I'm not sure I can get out of it."

"Agreed to what, exactly?" Gunther drew his brow down suspiciously as he set the practice swords away on the rack.

"Agreed to marry Prince Alexander? Or maybe it was the other one. I don't even know." Celine's voice rose to a wail. "I've never even met either of them. What should I do?"

"You agreed to do *what?*" Gunther's voice rose.

"Marry the prince... wait a minute, can I even agree to that? Maybe it's against protocol; maybe only Father can make those kinds of decisions. After all, there is an alliance involved." Celine's face brightened.

"That might be, but if you made it sound like a possibility to Queen Abigail, we're going to have to tread lightly. We just got back on good terms with the Iasians, and you know how we depend on the trade route that goes through here... Why are you always so impulsive?"

"I know, I know." Celine buried her head in her hands. "What should I do?" She peeked through her fingers, hoping for an answer.

Gunther ran his fingers through his thick, black hair. "We'll go along with it for now; if you see a way out, take it. I'll send a message to your father and let him know what's going on though."

"Do you really have to?" Celine rubbed the toe of her boot on the floor of the arena, kicking up a cloud of dust that itched her nose and eyes.

"Celine, you know I do." Gunther wiped his face with a cloth. "But we have time; we'll figure a way out of this while keeping the relationship intact. If anyone can sort this out, King Erich can." His words were encouraging, but his face told another story.

"But I wanted him to be proud of me." Celine watched Gunther leave the arena, before picking up another practice sword and launching into a series of lunges, stabbing the air again and again, until a sheen of sweat covered her skin. After finally exhausting herself, she sat, breathing hard, hoping that she hadn't started something that she couldn't mend.

CHAPTER ONE

Celine straightened the tiara on her head, wincing as its solid weight pinched her brow. Celine had tried *very* hard over the past several days to find an opportunity to break the news to Queen Abigail that she had no interest in being engaged to Prince Alexander, or any other prince for that matter. But every time she even got close to broaching the subject, Queen Abigail or King Ruben or even the friendly Prince Landry quickly changed the subject. Now, it was time for Prince Alexander to return and Celine *still* hadn't broken the news.

"You look lovely, your highness. You must be so excited." Sarah, the lady-in-waiting who accompanied Celine from Lovan, fussed with the hem of her buttercup hued gown. The colour matched the golden hair that flowed down her back, held back with pearl tipped pins.

"Oh, definitely. Very excited." Celine stretched a wide smile across her cheeks. She didn't want the royal family to find out about the non-existent engagement from the castle grapevine, so kept her feelings about the matter strictly between herself and Lord Gunther. As one of the most trusted members of her Father's council, she knew he would keep the matter discreet. She dabbed a bit of floral essence on her wrist and neck, letting the sweet scent warm against her skin.

After one last check in the mirror, Celine took a deep breath before straightening her spine and gliding into the hallway.

"I hope he doesn't like blondes," she muttered to herself. Her dearest hope was that Prince Alexander wouldn't be interested in her. The relief would far outweigh the sting of rejection, she decided.

Lost in thought, Celine didn't see the slight girl coming her way, lugging a heavy tray piled high with the remnants of an afternoon tea. Celine caught the edge of the tray with her elbow and sent the contents crashing to the ground, scattering broken dishes, crumbs, and cutlery across the floor.

"Oh, your highness," the girl's voice trembled, so frightened, she seemed on the verge of tears. "I am so sorry."

"Don't worry about it. I think it was my fault anyway, I should have looked where I was going." Heedless of her dress, Celine knelt to help the girl gather the crockery, brushing the broken shards onto an empty plate.

Tears welled up in the girl's eyes when she spotted a large patch of wet tea spreading on the silk of Celine's yellow gown.

"Oh, that." Celine dismissively brushed at the stain. "We can worry about that later. I never really liked this dress, anyway. Here, let me help you carry some of this. Were you on your way to the kitchen?" Ignoring the girl's protest, Celine took a haphazard pile of plates, ignoring the smear of chocolate sauce that joined the tea stain on her gown.

"But, your highness, you'll be late, and the party is for you." The girl tried to take the plates away.

"I insist." Celine led the way to the kitchen, finding out that the girl's name was Louise along the way. This was her first week working at the castle, and yes—she was indeed very glad that Queen Penelope left because Queen Abigail was lovely. After a few twists and turns, they arrived at the bustling kitchen where a red-faced cook, still holding a wooden spoon dripping with batter, met them.

"It wasn't her fault, it was mine." Celine flashed her most charming smile, trying to wheedle a bit of warmth out of the cook. "And it was such a shame, I saw the coconut meringues were on the tray. They're my favourite; I've been devouring them all week. You must send the recipe home with me. My mother would love them."

At this, the cook's face softened, "Off you go then, Louise. Make sure you don't leave any shards in the dishwater. They would cut your fingers, then where would we be?" She dismissed Louise with a nod. "Thank you, your highness." She bobbed a curtsy to Celine before turning back to the range.

Celine went back to her room and changed her dress, which made her very late to the dinner. Everyone had finished their first course, and the weight of every eye bored into her as she slid into her seat. "Sorry. I completely lost track of time." Celine flicked her hair back, smiling around the room. At the other end of the table, a pair of unfamiliar eyes met hers, their steady gaze unwavering. *That must be Prince Alexander.* Flustered at the intensity of his gaze, she looked at her plate, taking a spoonful of the delicate bisque set in front of her.

"Celine, this is my son, Prince Alexander." Queen Abigail confirmed Celine's suspicions as she gestured toward the dark-eyed stranger.

Celine swallowed, the delicious bisque suddenly turning in her stomach. "Lovely to meet you." She nodded toward the prince, trying not to notice the way his broad shoulders filled out his finely woven jacket. Suddenly unable to eat another bite, she set down her spoon.

After seven more courses, none of which Celine could do more than nibble on, it was time for dessert. Celine brightened up, knowing this meant she could soon escape to her room, away from the dark eyes that seemed able to pierce through her shield of pleasantness she put on in social situations.

"And now, for a toast." King Ruben stood, clinking his spoon against his glass. Celine's heart clenched in her chest, sending prickles of panic running up her spine. She hoped this wasn't going in the direction she suspected it would. "To the lovely Celine and our son, Prince Alexander. It's not official yet, but since we're among friends tonight, we want you to be the first to know.... this is the... ahem....

unofficial engagement." He raised his glass and beamed triumphantly at the twenty people sitting around the table.

Celine's heart sank, but she covered up her distress with a brilliant smile as she accepted the congratulations of the well-wishers. She raised her eyes to those of the dark-eyed stranger, who sat still as stone, an inscrutable expression on his handsome face. *He looks no more excited about this than I do.* She gave the prince a curious look, wondering for the first time if he was as surprised by this development as she was.

"And now, we will let the couple have their first dance together." King Ruben's voice broke into Celine's thoughts, snapping her out of her reverie. Celine pasted a smile on her face as she stood up, the silk layers of her deep red dress fluttering behind her as she floated toward the dance floor. Prince Alexander met her there, gravely offering his hand as they approached the dance floor together.

As the music played, they drifted out into the middle of the floor. Putting his hand around her waist, he leaned down and whispered. "I liked the yellow dress too."

Celine covered her surprise with a serene expression. He must have been in the hall earlier and seen her with Louise, the kitchen maid. "Thank you, it's one of my favourite colours," she whispered back as she swung out in a graceful spin before twirling back in again. Every eye in the room watched, glued to them as they swayed across the polished floor. He didn't speak to her again, and when the music ended, he bowed formally to her curtsey amid a smattering of polite applause. King Ruben and Queen Abigail smiled proudly. Celine quickly averted her eyes, finally settling them on Gunther, who gazed back, eyes full of worry. The dance floor soon filled with other guests, allowing Celine the chance to escape to Gunther's side.

"Did you know this announcement was going to happen?" she spoke out of the side of her mouth in a low voice, as she glanced around surreptitiously to make sure no one was close enough to overhear.

"No." Gunther shook his head with a frown. "I thought the plan was to keep it quiet until you had the chance to speak to your father. Are they so determined to make this marriage happen?"

"What are we going to do now?" Celine felt the panic edge into her voice.

"I don't know. The news will spread like wildfire now that everyone here knows. We'll just have to keep reiterating that it needs to go through the formal channels before it becomes official. Why didn't you speak to Queen Abigail sooner? I thought that was the plan."

"I tried." Celine rubbed her temple, a headache blooming. "She kept changing the subject. I think she knows I was caught off guard and have no intention of marrying the prince, but they're determined to go through with it anyway. If only Father had let me take part in more back at our court, I might have been on my toes a little more. And that's not all; I think Prince Alexander was spying on me. He told me he liked the yellow dress better."

"Yellow dress?" Gunther crinkled his brow.

"Yes. I had a yellow dress on earlier, but there was a mishap on the way to dinner; I had to change. He must have seen me."

"Well, if he was spying on you, he wouldn't have mentioned it. Did he say anything else to you, anything that might show how he feels about the alliance?"

"No. He didn't talk to me at all. I think he must hate me." Celine's shoulders drooped.

"We still have a few more days." Gunther consoled her. "We'll just have to keep looking for an opportunity to explain." As the music faded, people left the dance floor, leaving no more opportunity for discussion.

THE NEXT MORNING, AFTER an extra-long practice session, Celine wandered into the breakfast room only to learn that Prince Alexander had left the night before.

"He's gone away to our estate, left very early this morning," Queen Abigail explained as she spread marmalade on a slice of buttered toast. "There's so much to do now; we never had a chance to settle the estate and move our things since Penelope... left so suddenly. But I'm so glad you two met. It was lovely seeing you dance last night. Like a song." She dabbed at the invisible crumbs on her face with a starched linen napkin.

Celine piled her plate with scrambled eggs, sausages, and a mound of grilled mushrooms. "Oh, yes, about Prince Alexander—I was hoping to speak to my father when I get home. But in the meantime, are you sure it's a good idea that—"

"Oh dear, look at the time," Queen Abigail interrupted gaily as she stood up, leaving her half-eaten toast on the plate. "I'm supposed to meet with the seamstress about some curtains this morning. So busy settling into a new place. You must excuse me." She began to rush out of the room before Celine finished her sentence.

"Wait." Celine gathered all her courage, determined not to let Queen Abigail avoid the subject any longer. "I need to talk to you about the engagement."

"Of course, my dear." Queen Abigail sat back down in her seat, reluctance etching her pretty face.

Celine took a deep breath. She hated to make anyone unhappy, and she had a feeling what she was about to say was going to make Queen Abigail very, very unhappy. "I don't know if I'm ready to settle down just yet. I might need—more time."

"Of course, my darling. Take all the time you need." Queen Abigail reached out, patting Celine on the hand. "Ruben and I just got over excited about the whole engagement. I mean, you're *so* lovely, and of course, after everything with Queen Penelope, the alliance would be wonderful. After all, it was at the hand of your queen to be that she expired." Queen Abigail raised an eyebrow.

Celine gulped, one reason for her journey was to restore diplomatic relations after the disaster with Penelope. Even though Penelope was the one at fault, they couldn't afford isolation from their closest neighbours and allies. "Of course." She poked at a sausage with her fork. "A new alliance would be wonderful."

"I'm so glad you agree." Queen Abigail's face resumed its expression of calm. "Now, I really must be going. I do so hate being late for appointments."

CHAPTER TWO

Queen Abigail and King Ruben waved cheerily as Celine and her entourage left the castle gates. Celine rolled the tension from her shoulders; it had been a long, tense week. After relaying what Queen Abigail said, Gunther advised Celine to leave the situation to her father. "He won't make you do anything you don't feel comfortable with." The worry lurking in his eyes belayed his confident tone, and Celine could get rid of the worry that twisted in her gut.

Celine held her face up to the sunshine, enjoying the view of the countryside stretched out around her. She sat on Ginger, the whiskey-coloured mare she received as an eighteenth birthday present from King Erich and Queen Isabella. Celine preferred to ride—so much better than sitting in a stuffy carriage. Behind her, in the carriage, was Sarah, along with the collection of guards her father had sent for the trip.

"Is he going to be angry with me?" They were entering the border town of Harvin, their horses kicking up dust as they trotted down the main street. Celine glanced around. It was busier than usual, the thriving market square bustling with what appeared to be a carnival.

"I don't think *angry*," Gunther replied thoughtfully. "Maybe just worried. You know your happiness is his first concern. Erich's very good at diplomacy; he won't let them push him into anything he doesn't want to do. It was your first time, and considering that, this is forgivable—something was bound to happen. I just wish I hadn't let Abigail get you alone."

Celine sighed. "I just wanted everything to go right because it was my first time—oh look." She broke off mid-sentence and pointed to a woman in a sparkling gown who was standing barefoot on the back of a horse.

"Yes, it looks like there are some performers here. They probably came with the carnival." Gunther glanced over, uninterested.

"Performers? Why haven't we ever had them in for one of our events?" Fascinated, she took in the sights. To her left, a group of acrobats practiced their routine, contorting their bodies to fly through the air in a series of flips and twists.

"Well, sometimes the characters can be a bit unsavoury—try not to draw their attention." Drawing himself up in his saddle, Gunther kept his gaze firmly ahead as he rode on toward the inn in the centre of the town. "We'll have to stay indoors tonight and leave first thing in the morning."

As Gunther sped up his pace, Celine craned her neck, trying to get a better look. This was so unlike anything she had ever seen before. Out of the corner of her eye, she glimpsed a gilt-edged sign advertising a fortune teller. Leaving the horses in the courtyard with his men, Gunther ushered Celine and Sarah inside, away from the activity.

"So lovely to see you again," Henrietta, the innkeeper, came out of kitchen, wiping her hands on her apron. "We've made our chicken and dumplings tonight. And apple tart." She waved them toward a long wooden table in the centre of the cheery room. A crackling fire blazed in the fireplace, casting a warm, cosy glow over the tables.

Celine chose a seat with a view of the window where she watched a steady stream of people heading toward the market square. "What's happening out there?" she asked Henrietta, keeping her voice casual.

"The carnival is in town this week." Henrietta wrinkled her nose in disdain as she set down the steaming bowls of chicken and dumplings. A loaf of bread accompanied by a large knob of freshly churned butter followed. "Lovely for the children, although you have to keep an eye on anything not nailed down when they're around." Henrietta poured out mugs of cider from a jug.

"See? Unsavoury." Gunther took an enormous chunk of bread and spread it generously with butter. "Don't get any ideas in your head, you're staying in here where it's safe, young lady." He gave Celine a stern look, pulling down his bushy black eyebrows in a firm line across his forehead.

"Oh, of course not." Celine put on her most innocent expression as she took a bite of chicken, letting the rich gravy fill her mouth with its flavour. "In fact, I think I'm going to go have a rest. It's been such a long day." She faked a yawn as she stretched and headed for the stairs.

Gunther eyed her suspiciously as she left the room, followed by the loyal Sarah.

"I'm going out to see the carnival; I need to borrow a dress, one that won't draw too much attention." Celine sat on the narrow bed and began unlacing her velvet gown.

"But didn't Gunther tell us to stay in?" An anxious expression crossed Sarah's face. She hated bending the rules, one reason King Erich had sent her along with Celine in the first place.

"Yes, but what he doesn't know, won't hurt him. I'm just going to slip out for a few minutes. You know I can defend myself— not that I'll need to," she added quickly, seeing the panicked look on Sarah's face. "I just need to stay low, and I'll be fine." Celine rooted through a trunk, producing a nondescript grey dress. "This is perfect. But I'll have to take a knife or a dagger. A sword would definitely look suspicious under this." Celine continued to sort through the contents of the trunk, pulling out a small pearl-handled knife and a dagger. She stuffed one in her pocket and the other in a small bag she slung over her shoulder.

"You stay here and cover for me," she directed Sarah as she tucked her distinctive blonde hair into a cap. She added a handful of coins to the bag.

"But what will I tell Gunther if he asks where you are?" Sarah worried her lip as she watched Celine arrange some pillows under the blankets on the bed.

"Just tell him I fell asleep. He's far too much of a gentleman to come in for a closer look." Celine tossed Sarah a cheeky smile as she opened the window. Although it was on the second floor, there was a trellis strong enough to hold her weight. She pushed back the creaky shutters and eased her way down the trellis, leaving Sarah standing helplessly at the window.

A heady sense of freedom washed over Celine as she breathed in the scent of fried food and sweet, sugary pastries. Skipping after the crowd, she made her way through the town until she reached the square— now packed with villagers, finished with their day's labour. She spent a few minutes browsing stalls selling food and other merchandise before settling on a sweet concoction of fried dough sprinkled with cinnamon sugar. After finishing her treat, she leaned against a railing, licking the sugar off her fingers while watching a fire twirler spin his baton—a blur of golden flame against the evening sky. After a few moments, she moved on, weaving through stalls of merchandise. Spotting a crowd flocking around a performance, she drew closer.

Curious to see what the fuss was about, Celine pushed her way through the crowd. A young woman, only a girl really— modestly dressed save for the intricate copper neckplate circling her slender throat— had the crowd mesmerised. She stood motionless on a small wooden platform. Celine glanced up at the sign over it. Shifter, she wondered what that could mean—everyone knew real shifters were a mere fairy tale. A black-haired man at the base of the platform held a metal bowl half-filled with coins. Celine's keen eyes noted his velvet jacket, once fine, was worn and soiled in places.

"Parrot," called out a young boy; he threw a coin into a bowl. He looked up eagerly, excitement lighting up his face. Celine watched as the young girl closed her eyes, face drawn in concentration. With a flash of light and a puff of gritty smelling smoke, a large parrot flapped its wings where the girl had been standing a split second before.

Celine's eyes widened. There had been entertainment brought into the castle, but never anything like this. A moment later, another flash of light, and the girl once again stood before them. The crowd clapped as another customer stepped forward.

"A donkey." A young man stepped forward, putting his coin into the bowl. Another flash of light and that strange, gritty smell and a small grey donkey stood on the platform, nodding its head and swishing its stubby tail. The crowd cheered as the shape of the girl replaced the donkey, looking a bit pale, though none the worse for wear. After a few more changes, Celine moved on to the fortune-teller, ducking under the sign into the tent, stifling after the cool air.

"Hold out your hand, dearie." The fortune-teller, a tall woman with a lined face and dark, unbound hair spilling down her back, sat at a small round table. "I charge extra for the crystal." She nodded to a large shape covered by a black cloth. Celine assumed that must be a crystal ball.

"I don't need the crystal." Celine saved a few coins to get a trinket for Sarah. After all, she *was* very good about covering for her on this little adventure. She obediently held out her hand. A tingle ran up her arm at the woman's touch.

"Hmm... very interesting." The woman took Celine's manicured hand in her own rough one. She eyed the nails, buffed into smooth ovals. "I see you are from the nobility. I take it you've escaped your minders for the evening?"

"Yes." Surprised by the twinge of bitterness in the woman's voice, Celine wondered if seeing the fortune-teller was a good idea. The last thing she needed was to have her cover blown. They would never allow her out again. Now that the laws changed to allow mages and magic users to practice freely in Lovan, chances were, this woman was genuine. She tried to pull her hand away, suddenly aware that she was alone, and no one knew where she was.

"Well." The woman's stiff fingers gripped Celine's hand tightly before letting go. "I see you like adventures, but you feel trapped by recent circumstances. Stifled. But things are going to change soon. Very soon. You will need to be careful because people aren't what they seem."

"Thank you." Celine drew away her hand, clasping it tight. She drew out a coin and placed it on the table, avoiding the strange woman's touch.

"Don't worry, dear. I will not hurt you." The woman paused, lost in thought for a moment before speaking. "You're going to need this." The woman fished in the pocket of her voluminous patchwork skirt and fished out a key. Celine reached out for the tiny key— brass— noting the peculiar silver inlay embedded into its shank.

"Now, I believe I have another customer." The woman fixed her eyes behind Celine where the shadow of her next client fell across the entrance. Celine put the key in her pocket and turned to leave, ducking under the brightly embroidered sign over the fortune-teller's tent. She blinked a little, getting her bearings. Realizing it would be near dinner time, she headed back to the inn. Just as she was rounding the corner, a harsh voice stopped her in her tracks.

"I know your tired, but I paid good money to buy you, and you need to do your job." It was the man in the green velvet jacket, hovering over the young girl who had been performing on the stage earlier.

"But if I do too many, it drains me." The girl cringed, her face pale save the purple shadows under her eyes. "I don't know if I can keep it up for another two days. I need a rest and then I'll do whatever you want, I promise." Her eyes pleaded, luminous with tears.

"You need to keep it up. We've got a good gig here; it's the best it's ever been, and I don't want to hear anymore complaining." His voice was harsh, loud. Celine winced as he raised his hand to the girl, whipping her head back with the force of his blow as he struck her.

Tears ran down the girl's cheeks as she bowed her head, beaten into submission. "Now, you go out there, and you smile at them tonight—if you do your job right, I won't punish you anymore today. Then we'll talk."

Celine quickly slid behind the tent as the man turned, striding toward her. "Always complaining about something," he muttered, stooping into the fortune-teller's tent.

"Gerta!" he bellowed.

"Yes." The fortune-teller's voice was placid, calm.

"I don't want you putting ideas into that little brat's head. I did her a big favour taking her in like this. You know what was going to happen to her otherwise. And you—"

"I know," Gerta soothed. "But Karl, she's young, only coming into her skills. Go easy on her or you'll wear her out; you'd be making nothing from her then. And you know she's your best performer. Look, as long as she's got the collar on, she has to do what you want. Think about the long term; you want her earning for you three, five, even fifteen years from now. Give her time." Celine heard a rustle as Gerta's shadow moved across the tent.

"I suppose," Karl relented. "I'll think about it. But tonight, she has to work. I want to make a point that she has to do what we say when we say it. And like you said, you know what happens to magic users in Lovan when they're on their own; they'd eat her alive. She needs us more than we need her; we just have to remind her who's in charge." As Karl moved to leave, Celine slipped away, melting into the shadows as he emerged from the tent.

CHAPTER THREE

Celine squeezed through the window, scraping her leg on the sill as she clambered into the room. Sarah turned from the vanity where she was sitting, waiting for Celine's return. "Thank goodness you're back. I was getting worried." Her face was filled with relief.

Celine slid the window shut, then brushed a few stray leaves out of her hair. "I wasn't that long. Did Gunther even notice I left?"

"No, he knocked on the door once, but I did what you asked and told him you were sleeping. He seemed to be happy with that," Sarah admitted.

"Good." Celine peeled out of her clothes and began dressing for dinner. "I brought you something." She reached into the small bag and produced a silver hairpiece she bought from a vender at the fair. Delicate flowers were engraved along the edge of the comb.

"Thank you." Sarah took the piece, examining it with delight.

"I wish you could have come with me. It was amazing." Celine turned and lifted her waves of golden hair so Sarah could lace up her dress. "They had so many performers. Ones I've never seen before. *Magical* ones." She lowered her voice and spoke the last words in a whisper.

"Magic?" Sarah's eyes were wide. "What kind of magic?" Although the royal family had recently lifted the ban on practicing magic in Lovan, it still wasn't widely practiced or accepted—remaining on the fringe, frowned upon with suspicion by most of population. King Erich even had to send his army to put down riots in a few towns after he lifted the ban.

Celine sat at the vanity and let Sarah work the comb through her hair. "They had all the usual— the fire dancers, the acrobats, even a tightrope walker. But they had some that were definitely *real* magic as well." She paused, enjoying the attention as Sarah waited breathlessly for her to continue. "The best performer was the shapeshifter, a girl who could change form. Into any living thing you could think of."

"Really?" Sarah's voice was full of astonishment. "Anything, no matter how big or how small it was?" The comb stopped in Celine's hair as Sarah's eyes grew round.

"Anything." Celine nodded for emphasis. "But they were keeping her as a slave." A dart of anger flashed through Celine as she thought of the young girl trembling under Karl's onslaught of abuse.

Sarah's horrified eyes met Celine's in the mirror. "That's not even legal."

"I know." Celine nodded. "I overheard Karl, the man whose making her do the performances, speaking to the fortune-teller; they're just using her for entertainment to make money for themselves. Well, *he* is anyway. It was hard to know what she thought about the situation. I wonder if Father knows things like this are going on." She frowned, wondering if she should tell Gunther to send a few of her guards to free the girl from Karl's evil clutches.

"I know things aren't always great for people who have magic—that's why so few of them have come forward," Sarah admitted as she wound Celine's golden hair into curls, pinning each section into a crown around her head. "But your father would never allow slavery; you know well how he feels about that."

"I'm just worried that by the time I tell him, it will be too late for her." Celine toyed with her necklace as she leaned back in her seat.

"I'm not sure *we* can do anything about it." Sarah pinned the last curl, smoothing and patting it into place.

"Why not?" Celine's eyes gleamed as an idea occurred to her. "Why *can't* we do something about it? If I could get her out, we could take her back to the castle with us. We're only a day or two away at most. And with all those guards Gunther insisted on bringing along, there's no way they could fight us. We can bring her here tonight when everyone's asleep and leave first thing in the morning. Karl won't even know until it's too late." Her voice rose with excitement as she worked out her plan.

"Can't Gunther's men just go free her?" Sarah suggested.

"Yes." Celine bit her lip. She knew it was a wise suggestion, but the tug of adventure was too much to resist. "But, if they get involved, it might upset a lot more people. You know we can't just take her without causing a fuss. But if you and I go, we can just slip in and then right back out again. If you agree to come along, Gunther might let me go to the fair tonight. You know how he thinks you're sensible, and he's always in a better mood after a good dinner." She tripped over the words in her excitement. After all the long boring days of sitting at social events, the thought of doing something not only exciting, but useful was irresistible.

"Only if Gunther says we can go." Sarah relented. "And you know he probably won't. Didn't he call them *unsavoury?*"

"Thank you." Celine ignored Sarah's hesitation as she bounced to her feet and clapped her hands in delight. "You won't regret it."

Confident that she had gotten out of a potentially sticky situation, Sarah led the way as the two girls went down to dinner.

"I made this especially for you." Henrietta set down a large plate in front of Gunther— roasted meat on a bed of buttery mashed potatoes. Despite the copious number of treats Celine had devoured at the carnival, her mouth watered as she smelled rosemary and sage dressing smothered in rich gravy. Seating herself at the table, she pointed her most brilliant smile at Gunther.

"Feeling rested?" Gunther piled his fork high with a little of everything before shovelling it into his mouth, closing his eyes in bliss as he chewed.

"Yes, it was so lovely to have an afternoon off to rest." Celine lifted her fork and knife and cut daintily into her roast, being careful not to drip any gravy on her dress.

Gunther eyed her suspiciously but said nothing as he took another massive bite. "Delicious as always, Henrietta," he called out to the innkeeper, who beamed at the compliment. She brought another pitcher of gravy, pouring a generous helping over Gunther's food before setting it down.

Celine waited until Gunther emptied his plate and was digging his spoon into the pudding, a sticky concoction oozing in a puddle of golden syrup, before saying, "I was wondering if I might go for a stroll after dinner?" She wiped her fingers on her napkin. "Just for a bit of fresh air. Sarah can come with me." She fluttered her eyelashes.

"Well." Gunther cleared his throat as he took another bite of his pudding. "If you keep to the main street, you should be all right. I'll send a few of the men with you," he added a few lumps of sugar to his mug of tea.

"But aren't they tired?" Celine put on her most reasonable voice. "I don't think it's fair to make them do extra after all the traveling today, and it draws so much attention every time I take them anywhere. It's just I've never been to Harvin before, and I've heard it's such a lovely town. The main street is well lit, and the crowds have thinned." She glanced out at the street that cast a golden glow across cobblestones street.

Gunther leaned against the back of his chair, his bushy eyebrows lowering. "I suppose if you promise to keep to the main street and the market," he relented, seeing the pleading expression on her face. "Stay away from the carnival, though. I don't trust them. And if you're not back in an hour, I'm sending *all* the men after you. See what kind of attention you get then." He stirred milk into his tea and took a sip.

"I CAN'T BELIEVE HE let you talk him into this." Sarah grumbled as they strolled down the main street. Celine fingered the key the fortune-teller had given her as her sword swung at her side, Gunther insisted that if she wasn't going to take the guards, she should at least be armed as a precaution.

"You're going to love the fair." Celine had a skip in her step as the two girls approached the market. "We'll find the girl first and make a plan, then when it's safe, we'll get her out and bring her to the inn."

"Then what is she going to do when we get her there? You can't just let her fend for herself."

"Easy peasy. She can just come to the castle and stay with us. I'm sure if she wants a job, Daphne will have plenty for her to do." Celine dismissed Sarah's concerns with an airy wave of her hand. "Come on, I think the tents are this way. Get us some of those things first so we can blend it." Celine pointed at some sugary fried pastries skewered onto sticks.

After getting their pastries, Celine wove through the venders to the small platform where the girl had performed earlier. Seeing that the platform was empty, she looked around, wondering what her next step would be. A cluster of tents pitched at the far end of the square drew her eyes. They were not decorative like the fortune-teller's tent, but more practical affairs made of grey and brown canvas. It was clear whoever used them was treating them as a home. There was even a makeshift clothesline strung between two of the tents.

Celine drew up the hood of her cloak to avoid drawing attention, then the girls made their way toward the tents, stopping to look at the merchandise the venders had on offer along the way. Celine pretended to spot something beyond the tents and wandered past, peering around to search for the girl. There, inside the last tent, she saw her. The shadow of a slight girlish figure silhouetted through the thin canvas. "You stay here and watch," she lowered her voice and nudged Sarah, who was turning pale with nerves. "I think she's in that one." She used her chin to nod toward a canvas tent. Reluctantly, Sarah stood guard while Celine crept closer, making sure there were no curious bystanders.

"Pst..." she whispered to the girl who jerked her head up, big brown eyes rounded in surprise as she took in Celine's fine clothes. "What's your name?" Celine asked the girl, giving her an encouraging smile.

"They call me Cherry." The girl's voice was soft and sweet. She nervously fingered the long brown hair that fell down her back.

"I'm here to get you out of here." Celine stooped over and put her head in the tent, taking in her surroundings. Whatever financial success Karl had enjoyed at her expense was not shared. The tent was shabby, the canvas stained and frayed.

"Pardon?" A frightened look filled Cherry's big brown eyes.

"I'm getting you out of here," Celine whispered loudly. "Come on."

"But you can't." Cherry's lip trembled as she put her hand to the copper collar around her neck. "He put the collar on me. If I disobey him, it hurts."

"Can't you take it off?" Celine took a step closer.

Cherry shook her head. "He got it spelled. It only comes off with a key, and Karl carries it."

"This key?" Celine grinned as she slid the key the fortune teller had gifted her out of her pocket. It glittered in her palm.

"How did you get that?" The girl rose to her feet, a hungry expression in her eyes.

"It was a present. We will see if it works." Celine motioned with a finger for Cherry to turn around.

Cherry obediently turned her back to Celine, holding her hair up to expose her slender neck. Celine's hands shook with excitement as she fitted the tiny key into the mechanism on the girl's collar. With a shiver of energy that tingled through her fingers and up her arm, the latch to the collar snapped open with a tiny click.

"Come on, we have to hurry." Celine held out a hand and led the girl to Sarah, who was waiting with an extra cloak. "Keep your head down," Celine ordered Cherry, bundling her into the cloak. With Cherry safely sandwiched between them, they made a beeline back to the inn.

"Hey!" a loud, angry voice shouted behind them. "Where do you think you're going? She's mine."

"Oh no, it's *him*." Cherry's face paled as footsteps thundered behind them.

"Run," Celine shouted. "I'll stay here and take care of him." Not waiting to see if the girls followed her instructions, Celine swung around, her sword slithering from its scabbard as she took up a defensive position.

Sliding to a stop in front of her, the black-haired man eyeballed her raised sword. "So, it's like that, is it?" He raised an eyebrow as he reached for his own weapon, a wickedly curved scimitar. Realizing he was heavier and more powerful than she was, Celine knew she would have to depend on speed and skill if she wanted to hold her own against him.

Not waiting for him to attack, she struck first, dancing forward, the pointed edge of her weapon glinting as it skimmed the air. Lazily, the man batted her away, sending her backwards with a blow to her sword. Fear prickled at the back of Celine's neck, as her arm tingled with the force. He was far more well-trained than she thought. Mind racing, she darted forward again, this time going for his left side, his weak side she hoped. With a flick, he knocked her sword back, the clash of weapons ringing in her ears.

"Not going the way you hoped, is it?" His evil grin sent chills down her spine as he took another step forward, closing in on Celine. "I see you took my best money maker. Not nice." He tutted as Celine bravely held up her weapon, watching for an opening in his defense.

"No matter. I can think of other ways to make money. Say a princess look-a-like? I think people would pay to see that. Or maybe I could send a message to your father. I'm sure he'd pay a pretty penny to get his daughter back."

"You wouldn't dare." Celine took a step back and tripped over an uneven cobblestone, righting herself on shaking legs.

"No, I suppose that might be troublesome. But I'll need something to make up for the lost income; I might just take my chances." He narrowed his eyes and struck.

Celine barely blocked the blow which left her arm in agony from the force of its strike. She knew she couldn't fight him much longer. It was now or never; she gritted her teeth and sprang, propelling herself forward with all the speed she could muster.

"You little—" The scimitar clattered to the ground, skidding toward the gutter as the man clutched his arm, a patch of red spreading underneath his fingers.

Celine leaped forward, snatching up his weapon in one hand and holding the other one toward him. "Not today," she said, her voice even.

"Oy! What's happening?" a shout behind her caught the man's attention; his face filled with fear as he took in the sight of Gunther and his men closing the distance between them. Still clutching his arm, the man rushed down the nearest alleyway—Gunther's soldiers tearing after him in hot pursuit.

"I should have known you were going to get into trouble." Gunther took Celine by the arm, steering her back toward the inn. "Are you all right? He didn't hurt you?" He scanned her for injuries, relaxing when he saw she was still intact.

"I got him way worse than he got me." Despite Gunther's dour expression, Celine couldn't help but be proud of her accomplishment.

"Even so, I should have been there. Your father's going to have my hide before this trip is over; you won't be leaving your room again until I get you safely back to the castle," Gunther griped as he shepherded Celine toward the warm glow that spilled out of the doorway.

"I'm sorry. But really, it's all right. I was taking care of him just fine," Celine protested as she was guided inside and sat in a chair.

"Now, tell me everything. I need to know who I'm dealing with here." Gunther's voice was stern. He raked his hand through his thick black hair in exasperation.

Celine sighed, knowing there was no chance of getting away until Gunther was satisfied. "I found a girl who was being held against her will. I couldn't let that be on my conscience so I freed her."

"A girl?" Gunther lowered his bushy eyebrows. "Was that who came rushing in here with Sarah. Little thing about this tall?" He measured the air with his calloused hand.

"Yes. They were using her for her magic. I thought I was doing the right thing." Celine turned her big blue eyes to Gunther.

"The right thing would have been coming to me first." Gunther grumbled. "You know we wouldn't allow that here if we found out about it."

"I know." Celine slumped back in her chair. "But that takes *so long*. And the girl needed help now. They were mistreating her; you know I can't allow that."

"I'm still going to have to tell your father. And this girl will be your responsibility. Did you even have a plan of what you were going to do with this girl once you freed her?"

"She can go back to her family." Celine shrugged. "Or come back to the castle with us if that doesn't work, we'll think of something."

Gunther exhaled loudly. "You can't just take in every stray you find; the castle would burst at the seams in no time."

"Well then, something else has to change." Celine set her face stubbornly. "And we're going to have to do something about the way they treat people when they have magic. It can't go on like this forever; it's not fair." She pressed her lips together.

"You can't change people overnight, even it is the right thing. But I suppose you have a point. We'll take her to the castle with us, then I'll talk to King Erich when we get there. Now, no more jaunts; we're leaving first thing in the morning, and I want no more incidents while you're in my care. Your father will never trust me again." Gunther gave her one last warning look before leaving the room, muttering under his breath.

Celine straightened her shoulders. That wasn't nearly as bad as she expected. Now, if she could just get through the conversation about the pseudo-engagement with Prince Alex, her life would be smooth sailing again.

CHAPTER FOUR

The wooden door creaked as it opened. Henrietta had improvised a bed in the corner of the room for Cherry who was settled in an armchair chair, being plied with tea and buns. She raised her eyes, looking timidly through her lashes when Celine came through the door.

"Did you get Karl?" Cherry asked, setting down a half-eaten scone slathered in cream.

"No, he got away." Unwilling to wait for morning to learn the outcome of the chase, Celine had checked in with Gunther's men to find out what had happened to her would-be abductor. "They said it was like he disappeared into thin air. Is that his power?"

Cherry swallowed the bite of scone. "I don't know. He didn't like us to know too much about him, and he kept to himself when he wasn't minding us. The only person he talked to was Gerta, and he didn't trust her either. Not really."

"Did he work alone, I mean, when he wasn't with the performers?" Hungry for any useful information, Celine pressed the matter.

"No." Cherry crinkled her brow as she thought. "I never saw any of the others, but I heard them talking sometimes—they came to his tent a few times. I think at least one of them had an estate in the country."

"Them?" Celine asked.

"Him and Gerta—the fortune-teller."

"But, if she's working with him, why did she give me the key?" Celine sat on the bed and unlaced her boots.

"I don't think Gerta really liked him; she just knew how to stay on his good side. And I have no idea how she would have gotten the key—he always had it around his neck. But Gerta is mysterious; she has her own reasons for doing everything. I've known her for a long time."

"And is the fortune-telling real? Is she an actual seer?" Celine pulled off a boot, setting it aside before she loosened the laces on the other one.

"She told me once she sees possibilities and likelihoods, but people are always free to make their own choices and change the outcome." Cherry helped herself to another scone, scooping a blob of lemon curd over the flaky dough.

Celine leaned back against the pillows, putting her hands behind her neck. "It just doesn't make sense that she would do that," she murmured, mind spinning with possibilities.

CELINE SHIFTED ON HER horse as they approached the castle. Her nerves had increased with each mile they drew nearer to the capital city of Cardon. What were King Erich and Queen Isabella going to say when they found out how dismally she had failed at her first attempt of diplomacy? She hated disappointing her parents. Her hands tightened on the reins as the castle gates loomed in front of her. A guard saluted smartly as he hauled them open, allowing the party to pass through.

"Will you come with me when I give my report?" she asked Gunther in a whisper as they clattered into the courtyard.

"Of course. Just give me an hour to debrief the men," Gunther's voice was kind. He swung down from his mount and handed the reins to a waiting groom.

Relieved by his offer of support, Celine dismounted and turned to Sarah and Cherry, who were disembarking from the carriage. "Can you get Cherry settled? I'm going to see Father and Mother."

"Of course." Sarah smiled and held out a hand to Cherry, who was staring at the teeming activity in the courtyard with a timid expression in her eyes. Celine left the girls and went up to her room, flopping on her bed with a groan. Even with Gunther's offer of help, she was dreading the next few hours. A soft knock at the door interrupted her thoughts.

"Come in." The door opened, and Cherry's big brown eyes peeked around the edge of the wooden panel.

"Cherry?" Celine flung back her long golden hair as she smiled politely. "Did Sarah introduce you to Daphne? She's the head housekeeper so she'll find a room for you."

"Yes." Cherry's voice was sweet. "I just thought you might need some help in here. I could unpack your things for you—unless you don't want me to." She bit her lip.

"No, of course, that would be lovely." Truthfully, Celine would have preferred a few moments to herself, but hated to hurt the girl's feelings. She looked so scared and shy. "They'll bring the trunks up shortly, so we can unpack later. But in the meantime, can you do my hair? I have a meeting soon and need to get ready." She gestured ruefully towards her clothes, which were a bit dishevelled after the day's travel.

"Oh, yes. I used to do Gerta's hair all the time." Cherry's eyes lit up as she stepped inside the room.

Celine took a seat at the vanity as Cherry picked up the silver brush and stroked it through her hair, working out the tangles. "Were you with Gerta long?" Celine kept her voice conversational, as she relaxed under Cherry's ministrations.

"A few years. My mother and father died in the riots, and Gerta took me in. She was an old family friend."

"But then how did you get mixed up with..."

"Karl?" Cherry lowered her lashes. "Gerta was just getting by before the riots, but things were terrible after. We had to move away and when Karl offered her an opportunity with the carnival, she thought it was the best thing for both of us." Cherry shrugged as she began pinning Celine's tresses onto the top of her head. "Gerta was good to take me in, but I suppose I was a bit of a burden to her." Her eyes were sad in her thin face.

"But wasn't she angry when Karl put that collar around your neck and made you perform?" Celine gaped, shocked at the fortune-teller's apparent callousness.

"Oh yes. She tried to stop him; I heard her arguing about it with him a few times. But she was frightened. Karl is very... strong, and Gerta didn't have anywhere else to go. You know how people are about magic in Lovan—not that it's your fault," she added quickly. "Just because it's not outlawed anymore doesn't mean people like it—or the people who can use it." A note of bitterness entered her voice. "Karl knew if we didn't have him on our side, there was a good chance we would have starved or worse."

Celine turned around in her seat, putting her hand on Cherry's shoulder. "Well, you're safe here. If anyone does anything to you, just let me know; I'll have something to say about it." A fierce expression crossed her face.

"Thank you." A faint pink stained Cherry's pale cheeks. She drew back as a loud knock sounded on the door.

"My trunks are here." Celine stood up, patting her hair. A bit outdated, she thought, looking at the simple style, but it would do for her mother and father.

"If you just help me with my dress, Sarah can show you where to put everything when she gets back." With Cherry's help, Celine quickly changed out of her travel-stained clothes, donning a floaty dress of soft blue silk. Her sister-in-law, Lucie, had done wonders for court fashion, bringing in her own unique sense of style mixed with elegant, easy fitting fabrics. Sliding her feet into her slippers, Celine left Cherry in the room and glided toward the royal apartments where her father and mother were waiting.

"Father? Mother?" Celine opened the heavy panelled door. Gunther had already arrived, lounging back in a leather chair with a cup of tea and a slice of iced cake in hand.

"Hello, darling." Queen Isabella, usually so poised and calm, ran to meet her, squeezing her daughter so tightly she gasped for air. "We missed you." She pulled back, looking at her daughter's face, so like her own.

"Hello, poppet, nice to have you back again." King Erich, a big blonde bear of a man, greeted her from his seat by the fire. Even Queen Isabella's little dog, Fifi, yipped and pawed around her ankles, begging for a cuddle.

"Hello, Father." Celine lifted the tiny dog and settled her in her lap, sneaking her a crumb of cake from the plate her mother offered.

"You will give the full report to the council tomorrow," King Erich began. "But a rundown first would be nice. How did everything go?" His deep voice rumbled through the room. Celine flinched. Her father was the kindest man she knew, and she hated to disappoint him.

Celine gulped. "*Mostly* all right," she began, hoping her news wouldn't be too disturbing to her mother and father. "But there was one teeny tiny thing that went wrong."

King Erich raised an eyebrow, waiting for her to continue. "Queen Abigail seems to think that I want to be engaged to Prince Alexander."

"Seems to think?" Queen Isabella questioned.

Celine sighed, knowing she would have to tell them the full story. "It happened when we were having tea. It was so boring, and I got distracted, and that's when I agreed to... to marry Prince Alex without even meaning to." Her big blue eyes widened emotion. "I know it's my fault—but when I asked if they could keep it quiet until I told you first, they made an announcement to all their friends." She pouted with annoyance.

"But why didn't you just tell them you didn't mean it?" King Erich furrowed his brow.

"I started to—once—but she started talking about Penelope, implying it was our fault she died. She knew I wasn't thrilled about the engagement, but she was determined to make it happen, anyway."

"And Prince Alexander, what does he think of the engagement?" Queen Isabella leaned forward, concern in her eyes.

"I don't even know." Celine rubbed her hand on Fifi's soft white fur. "I only saw him once, and he barely even spoke to me."

King Erich leaned back thoughtfully, steepling his hands under his chin. "Well, if Abigail thinks she can bully you-us into an engagement just to create an alliance, she needs to think again. That's not how we do things in Lovan."

"But what are we going to do? I don't want to be the one responsible for us *not* having an alliance. She even reminded me of how much we need the Iasians for our trade routes." Despite the relief that flooded her when hearing King Erich's response, Celine's eyes were shadowed with worry. She would hate to cause problems between the two kingdoms.

King Erich waved a hand, dismissing her concern. "They need us as much as we need them. Ruben and Abigail know their way around the court. After all, he was the duke long before he became king. But they can't throw their weight around like that. Taking advantage of you like that when you're young and green just isn't fair." King Erich set his mouth in a firm line. "If you *wanted* to get engaged to Prince Alexander, it would be a completely different matter of course. We would be delighted. But we would never force you into a marriage. Not after what happened with Frederich. And to be honest, we're working on ways to be less dependent on the Iasians for trade. This just confirms what I thought all along. We need to diversify our trade routes."

For the first time in over a week, Celine felt the knot of apprehension in her chest relax. Things were going to be all right. She took a bite of lemon cake, her appetite suddenly returning.

"Hello sis," a voice behind her interrupted Celine's thoughts.

"Lucie?" Fifi scrambled for cover as Celine leapt up, nearly tipping over the plate. Delighted, she turned to her sister-in-law. "And what about Frederich? Is he coming too?"

"He's working at the harbour today." Lucie rolled her eyes. "Again. He can't stay away from the ships. He's dying to see you though; he said he'll be here for dinner. Not that I'll be eating anything." A pleased look crossed her face.

"Why not... Oh." Celine looked down to where Lucie's hands were cradling her non-existent belly. "Are you?"

Beaming, Lucie nodded. "I couldn't wait to tell you."

Overcome with joy, Celine gave Lucie another tight squeeze. "I can't believe I'm going to be an aunt. I can't wait."

Still brimming with happiness after a lovely dinner with her family, Celine returned to her room, humming a tune. She opened the door to see Cherry start back from the vanity, dropping her hairbrush on the polished wooden surface with a clunk.

"Oh, you startled me." Cherry put her hand to her chest.

"I'm so sorry, I didn't mean to frighten you." Feeling oddly wrong-footed, Celine apologized, although why she should apologize for coming into her own room she didn't know.

"I was just tidying up a bit." Cherry moved the hairbrush to a different position on the vanity.

"You can have a rest if you like." Celine sat down to remove her slippers. She had been looking forward to spending a few moments alone.

"Oh no, your highness, I'm all right. " Cherry fidgeted with a collection of crystal bottles, adjusting them on a silver tray. "I like to help."

"I'm going to get ready for bed now. Has Sarah shown you a room?" Celine pretended to yawn as she glanced around the room, wondering what Cherry had been doing in there. The room didn't look any different from what it usually did, and the trunks were still sitting by the bed, unpacked.

"Yes, your highness, a very nice one. I just sent for some hot chocolate for you to drink. Sarah said you like to take it before bed." Cherry moved to the bed and folded back the covers.

"Hot chocolate would be nice." Celine forgot her annoyance as her heart warmed at the girl's thoughtfulness.

"I'll just see if it's ready." Cherry moved to the door, leaving Celine to change into the lacy nightgown laid out on the bed.

Tucked up under the coverlet, Celine sipped at the hot chocolate, frowning a little at the bitter aftertaste that lingered on the back of her tongue. "Is there a different cook in the kitchen?" She wrinkled her nose. "This doesn't taste like it usually does."

"I'm not sure, your highness." Cherry's doe eyes took on a worried expression. "Would you like me to find out? I can get you another one?" She moved as if to take the cup from Celine's hand.

"No, no, this is fine." Celine took a large gulp, not wanting to offend Cherry, who was fidgeting and anxious again. She finished the drink and set it on the silver tray. Her eyes drooped, and she yawned, settling her head on the pillow as Cherry gently removed the tray, closing the door softly behind her as she left the room.

CHAPTER FIVE

Celine's head ached as her mind dragged itself back into consciousness. She forced her gritty eyelids to crack open, wincing as the piercing light flooded her senses. Slowly, slowly, she peeled her head off the pillow. It felt strange, light. Raising her hand to the crown of her head, she froze in shock. Last night, there had been cascades of golden waves tumbling down her back; today, there was only a fine scratchy stubble. With a cry of distress, her other hand flew to her head, clutching at her naked skull. Frantically, her eyes darted around the room. Everything seemed normal; someone had pulled the curtains back, allowing sunshine to spill across the soft carpeted floor. Her eyes searched the room, looking for anything out of place, finally landing on the figure of a girl sitting in an armchair near the window.

"What's happening?" Celine forced the words out of her dry mouth.

"Ah.. you're awake." The girl set aside the book she was paging through. "I thought I maybe gave you too much. I'm not really used to using potions; it would be *so* easy to slip up."

Celine's bleary eyes focused on the girl. She had a slight figure, wide startlingly blue eyes, and a waterfall of golden hair. She realized with a start, it was exactly like looking into a mirror. "Who *are* you?" she breathed, letting the bedclothes fall into a heap as she flung them aside.

"I'm Celine, of course." The girl smiled a wide, toothy grin full of gleaming white teeth as she sauntered across the room, running a hand down the length of her hair.

"But—it's not possible." It dawned on Celine that it was possible, but the *why* escaped her. "Cherry? You're the only one who could do this. But why?" Her voice was pleading.

"Why?" Cherry scoffed. "Why *wouldn't* I want to be you. A pampered princess who everyone loves so much. Especially when the alternative is to be stuck here as some kind of servant for the rest of my life. I'm not any better off here than I was with Karl. Eventually, someone would find out what I can do, and I'd end up right back where I started." She spit out the words, eyes hard.

"You can't possibly think this is going to work." Celine narrowed her eyes as the fog lifted. "You might look like me, but you can't act like me. They're going to notice."

"Will they?" Cherry raised an eyebrow, no hint of her former timidity in sight. Her face took on a delighted, happy expression as she bounced across the room in a parody of Celine, swishing her dress. "Oh look, my favourite new dress. I'm so excited." Her voice was high and mocking, but Celine had to admit, it sounded a bit like her.

"Well, I'll just tell them it's me." Heedless of the fact that she was still wearing a nightgown, Celine bolted for the door.

"I don't think you want to do that." Quick as a flash, Cherry was standing in front of Celine, barring her way. Her blue eyes cold, she glared at the other girl. "Look at yourself." She grabbed Celine by arm and pushed her toward the mirror. Celine's heart sank at the unfamiliar sight that met her eyes. Not only had the distinctive waves of blonde hair been stripped from her head, leaving her like a shorn sheep; her features had completely morphed overnight into something completely unrecognizable. Mud coloured eyes peered out from behind sparse, scattering eyelashes. Celine saw her button nose had grown into a monstrosity that resembled an overgrown potato more than a nose.

"What have you done to me?" Celine's hands flew to her cheeks, which were red and swollen, her smooth skin replaced by a rough scaly texture.

"Oh, that." Cherry waved a hand. "That's from the hot chocolate. Very greedy of you gulping the whole thing in one go like that. You should really be more careful." Cherry leaned forward to admire her own visage in the mirror, smoothing her golden locks with pride.

"You know they will find out, eventually. And when they do, it won't be good for you." In desperation, Celine tried reasoning with the other girl. "If you change me back right now, I promise to ask them to go easy on you. We don't even have to tell anyone." She raised her pleading eyes to Cherry.

Cherry smirked. "They won't find out. Because I don't intend to be here for much longer. I've decided that I do want to marry prince Alexander after all. In fact, I intend to announce it to the council this morning."

Celine gaped at the other girl, her mouth hanging open like a fish.

"I think I want a brief engagement," Cherry continued in a sickening voice, smoothing her hands down the front of her dress. "They're so much more romantic, don't you think? You see, no one will suspect me in Iasia; they don't know you all that well. I'm going to be Princess Celine forever." She turned to the other girl, eyes gleaming triumphantly.

Black spots swam before Celine's eyes as she realized her future was disappearing in front of her. Taking a deep breath, she screamed for the guards, the sound wrenching out from deep within.

"Oh, I think you've made a big mistake there." Cherry gloated as she glided across the floor, silk dress rustling like petals around her. Footsteps pounding down the corridor and a trio of guards burst through the door.

"There." Cherry pointed her finger at Celine, a calculated expression of fear pasted across her face. "This girl came into my room and threatened me. I was so frightened." She gave the closest guard a beseeching look, tears swimming in her ocean blue eyes. "If you hadn't arrived, I don't know what I would have done."

"No, *I* called you." Realising she was still in her nightgown, Celine crossed her arms in front of her chest self-consciously.

"You?" The guards turned to her in confusion. "Who are you? And what are you doing in princess Celine's room?" He grabbed her by the arm, his hand an iron band around her arm.

"I don't know where she came from." Cherry's lip trembled as she batted her long lashes at the guard. "I just turned around and there she was. You don't think she's dangerous, do you?" She lowered her voice and edged closer to the guards.

"But she's not Celine. I am," Celine insisted, a gut-wrenching sense of futility creeping into her heart. Who was going to believe her now, looking like this?

"Your highness, what would you have us do with her?" The guards turned to Cherry, waiting for instructions.

"Check her for weapons, then banish her from the city. I don't think she actually wanted to hurt me. Although you might want to check your security procedures. It wouldn't do for my father to know you let someone slip right into my room like this." A hint of imperiousness entered Cherry's voice as the threat rolled off her tongue.

"Yes, your highness." Celine whimpered as the guard gripped arm, jerking her toward the door. Surprised by the rough treatment, Celine gave a squeak of pain as, still in her bare feet and nightgown, they dragged her between them, down the corridor toward the back entrance of the castle.

CHAPTER SIX

Celine's mind raced as they rounded the corner of the long corridor leading toward the kitchen. She knew she had one chance to slip free, but her timing would have to be perfect. When they passed the statue or her grandfather, she took it. Catching them by surprise, she let her body go limp, using her weight to force them to slow down. The guard on her left, a bull-like man, paused, giving her the opportunity she was waiting for. She sprang up, kicking out with all her strength. He grunted in surprise when her foot glanced off his thigh, loosening his grasp. Making the most of her extensive training, she twisted away from the other guard, and rolled under his grasping hands then darted back to the statue, whipping aside a large tapestry of a battle scene in the alcove behind, sliding into a hidden recess in the back wall.

Celine held back a sneeze as she squeezed into the tiny opening behind the tapestry. Curling herself into a tiny ball, she pressed herself tight against the wall, forcing her breath to quiet when she heard the guards shouting and scuffling mere feet away. The secret passage was unknown to most of the castle residents, only the royal family and a select few members of the king's most elite guards were even aware of its existence. When the voices faded away, rushing off into the distance, Celine fumbled through pitch darkness, feeling for the latch to the tunnel. The door was always closed tight, so the drafts wouldn't give away the location of the tunnel. Inch by inch, she lifted the ancient latch, hoping it wouldn't creak and give her away. At last, the door swung open, a cool draft caressing Celine's hot cheeks as she melted into the bowels of the castle.

The extensive web of tunnels led to all the royal apartments, including her father's council chambers, the armoury, and even the kitchens. Anything they needed to access in case of attack was accessible by the intricate system. *And this is an attack,* Celine thought grimly, rubbing a hand on her shorn head. She put her hand on the damp wall, shuddering at the spiderwebs that clung to her fingers as she crept down the twisting tunnel toward the royal apartments. It was early enough that her mother and father would still be at their breakfast.

The corridors were lit but just barely, by small airholes drilled through the stone at intervals. On the other side, paintings and tapestries covered the holes, fading seamlessly into the castle walls. Over the years, Celine and Frederich had spent hours in the tunnels, first as part of their training and next as a running series of practical jokes. Celine had taken great delight in jumping out at him when he was unaware. She grimaced, little did she know their childish games would turn out to be so useful.

A frenzy of high-pitched barking guided her to the royal apartments. Fifi must be in a strop, unusual for the placid little dog but not unheard of. Celine peeked through the hole in the wall, her vision blocked by the small size of the opening. She could only see the back of Lucie's head and the corner of her father's chin.

"Fifi. What has gotten into you?" Queen Isabella scolded the small dog. "Don't you remember Celine after her trip? She hasn't been away that long." Fifi growled in response, not convinced by Isabella's persuasion.

"It must be the new perfume I got while I was away." Cherry protested in her best impersonation of Celine's voice. Celine rolled her eyes as Fifi growled again. After a scuffle, she heard a door close, and the barking muffled. Queen Isabella must have removed her from the room.

"That dog." Her mother came into view, passing only a foot or two away from Celine's position at the wall. "I just don't know what got into her. She only saw you last night."

A tinkling laugh that must be Cherry and scraping chair let her know someone was sitting down. "I'm sure she'll come around." Cherry seemed unconcerned that the family pet had forgotten her. "But no matter, I really just came to tell you my news."

"News?" King Erich's pleasant voice rumbled. Celine heard utensils clinking as the family resumed their meal.

"Yes. I've decided to marry Prince Alexander."

A thump sounded as a coffee cup thudded to the table. "Are you sure about this? Last night you were determined to have nothing to do with him. You don't have to do this just for the alliance; you know we would never sacrifice you like that." Queen Isabella's voice was reasonable, but Celine heard the confusion in her voice.

"I think it's a splendid opportunity for us to cement the alliance for good. And he is very handsome." Another tinkling laugh.

I don't giggle like that. Celine thought, glaring at the tiny hole in the wall. She wished she could see Cherry's face.

"Well, don't jump into it, take some time to at least think about it," King Erich insisted. "How about if we discuss it again after the council meeting?"

"But wouldn't the council meeting be the best time to tell them?" Cherry's honeyed tone wound round the room. "I'm sure they would be delighted if we could restore the alliance."

Ice trickled down Celine's spine as she realized Cherry was putting her plan into place sooner rather than later. If she wanted to make her presence known, it would have to be now. She took a deep breath, gathering the courage to say her piece quickly before Cherry could sway their opinion. A knock at the door cut her off.

"Your Majesty." It was Nathanial, captain of the guard. "I'm here to report a disturbance in the castle. A security breach has left an unknown person within the walls."

"Do they mean us any harm?" King Erich was alert.

"We're not sure of their intentions yet. However, we found the woman in question in Celine's room this morning. She didn't seem lucid. It gave your highness quite a fright."

"Is this true Celine?" King Erich's voice was serious.

"Yes, Father." Cherry's voice was demure. "I thought they caught her, though. They took her away before I came to breakfast."

"Unfortunately, the woman is well trained. She slipped past the guards and escaped. They gave chase, but she disappeared, and we still haven't tracked her down. We believe she may be dangerous." Nathaniel's clipped voice seeped through the walls, filling Celine's heart with ice. She knew she couldn't get caught now, not if she wanted to stop Cherry before she left for Iasia.

"Put everyone under double guard until we apprehend her," King Erich decided, leaving no room for objections. "Since she was in the princess's chambers, I consider her a grave danger to the crown; you have my permission to defend by whatever means necessary." Celine nearly gasped aloud, pressing herself tighter against the wall. This recent development left no opportunities for Celine to explain herself before finding herself at the wrong end of a sword.

"Thank you, Father." Celine cringed at the simper in Cherry's voice. That was *not* how she talked. Ever. Gritting her teeth, her mind raced to form a plan. There had to be some way of getting out of this mess.

CELINE MELTED INTO the darkness as she silently crept along the tunnel toward the meeting room. She was still barefoot, having no opportunity to get shoes. The grit underfoot rubbed against the soles of her feet. Before making a plan, she had to see what Cherry was up to, and the council meeting was her best chance to find out. She pressed one eye to the beam of light that filtered through the hole in the wall. This viewpoint was significantly better than the one in the royal apartments— located above the council room, giving Celine a bird's-eye view of the entire room. She settled to wait, watching as the steward arrived to prepare the room for the meeting, bringing in plates of sandwiches and trays of pastries along with a selection of hot and cold drinks. Queen Isabella prided herself on her hospitality and reminded Celine more than once that people never made good decisions on an empty stomach.

The council members trickled in, their footsteps muffled by the thick rugs covering the floor. After helping themselves to the refreshments, they took their seats around the long, polished table that stood in the centre of the room. Celine's stomach growled as the buttery scent of hot pastries floated up. Because of all the commotion, there had been no chance of breakfast. She put a hand to her stomach, hoping they wouldn't hear it grumbling over the murmur of conversation.

After what felt like hours, the door finally opened and in glided Celine, followed by King Erich and Queen Isabella, who took their places in the high-backed chairs at the head of the table.

King Erich cleared his throat, and the murmur faded to a hum as the members of the council turned to listen. "Celine will give us her report of the diplomatic visit to Iasia before we begin our usual proceedings." He nodded at Cherry, giving her the floor.

"Good morning." Cherry plastered a wide smile across her face. "First, I am pleased to tell you all that the diplomatic visit was a success." She beamed around at the council members. "In fact, I have secured an alliance with Iasia—one that will hopefully be long and prosperous."

"An alliance?" Gunther lowered his bushy brows questioningly as he fastened his eyes on Cherry.

Good, thought Celine from her perch. Gunther knows I hated the whole marriage idea. Maybe he can get them to realize that it's not me down there.

"Yes." Cherry fluttered her eyelashes in his direction. "I reconsidered— really thought about it— and I decided that I *will* accept the offer of an engagement and marry Prince Alexander." Again, came the glittering smile. "I plan to travel to Iasia as soon as possible to begin the arrangements." At this announcement, the council members exchanged disapproving looks. Celine leaned forward. She knew most of the council members were older and set in their ways. They would be cautious about rushing into anything.

Celine looked directly underneath her to where her father and mother were sitting; it was hard to see their faces from the angle she was, but she saw her father's hand grip his cup until his knuckles whitened. Queen Isabella sat still and poised as always, but Celine could see by the slight tremble of her fingers that this announcement also shocked her.

"I'm sorry, Father—Mother,"Cherry turned to the king and queen. "I know you wanted me to wait, but I'm just so excited, I had to share it with everyone." She batted her lashes at the council members.

"But the contract? When will that be written?" Jean Paul, one of Father's oldest and most experienced council members, spoke up. "This is unheard of without a proper negotiation." He took off his glasses and polished them.

"Yes, I thought you were going to wait until we could discuss it further." Prince Frederich spoke from his seat at the other end of the table. Celine held her breath, hoping her brother would talk some sense into the girl. She needed some time to fix the situation before getting married off to the nearest suitor, even if he was a prince.

"I know it's not protocol." Cherry widened her big blue eyes. "I am very sorry. I didn't mean to offend anyone. But when it comes to matters of the heart, sometimes protocol comes second."

"Are you sure this is what you want?" Father turned to the Cherry.

"Yes, Father, I've never been more sure of anything in my life."

"It would make things easier if we had that kind of alliance," Jean Paul spoke up again. "There's nothing stopping us from drawing up our terms now. We can send them ahead by messenger and begin the negotiation process."

"And just think of all the opportunities we would have to learn how they operate their mage guilds. I'll have to discuss some opportunities about this with you later." Lord Remy's eyes glinted with excitement behind his thick spectacles.

No, no, no. Celine glared at the top of Cherry's golden hair, unable to believe what was happening below. Eye glued to the tiny hole, she watched in disbelief as one by one she swayed them, reeling them in with the prospect of a rich trade deal with Iasia. Only her father, mother, brother and of course, Gunther seemed to have real reservations regarding the matter. But even they eventually gave in on the condition that Cherry give them two weeks before making the journey back to Iasia. Finally, the meeting was over. Celine drew back into the murky depths of the tunnel, heart aching. Two weeks. Two weeks to get her freedom and her identity back. She rested her head in her hands, wondering how she would ever accomplish this impossible task.

Celine tipped her head back, leaning against the rough wall of the tunnel. Her mind turned over various options. The most obvious would be to convince someone she was the real Celine and not that imposter so ruthlessly determined to take over her life. Frederich. She decided Frederich would believe her, he had to. After all, they had so much shared history that Cherry knew nothing about. Now, if she could only get him alone. She stooped under a small archway that led to the royal apartments and swiftly found her way to the library. Her sister-in-law, Lucie, was a bookworm and loved to have a bit of time in her favourite part of the castle after a trying council meeting. And where Lucie went, Frederich liked to follow.

She peeked around a stack of dusty smelling books that blocked the entrance to the library.

There she was, curled up in a patch of sunshine on a settee. Lucie flipped through the pages of her novel and sipped at her hot tea. The fire blazing in the hearth offered a cozy warmth; she had kicked off her slippers, leaving them sprawled across the floral rug that lay on the floor. Silently, Celine tiptoed toward them, crouching behind a shelf to avoid being seen.

"Did you think there was something a bit odd about Celine this morning?" Frederich tapped his fingers together thoughtfully.

Lucie lowered her book, peering over the top of the thick volume. "What kind of odd? I mean, your sister was always a bit impulsive."

"Yes, but she rarely changes her mind so suddenly. She just finds creative ways to get what she wanted all along."

"And you don't think she wants to marry Prince Alexander? I've heard he's lovely and very handsome."

"She wasn't at all interested last night; and today she was bound and determined to leave the minute she could get away. She just seemed.... *off.*" Frederich narrowed his eyes.

"She's probably just getting accustomed to being back home again. She's had a taste of independence now, and maybe she thinks this is what she needs." Lucie poked her nose back into the book, licking her finger and flicking a page.

Celine knew this was her chance. Taking a deep breath, she smoothed her hands down her now grubby nightgown and poked out from her hiding place. Not recognizing Celine, Lucie yelped in surprise at the sight of the dishevelled girl. Frederich sprang up from his seat, ready to defend his wife.

"Wait, Frederich, it's me. CeeCee." Celine used her childhood nickname, hoping that would convince him.

Frederich froze for an instant, taking one disbelieving look at her unkempt appearance and spiky bald head before shouting for guards. He reached for the poker and held in front of him and his pregnant wife, waving it back and forth protectively.

"Just listen to what I have to say for one minute." Celine held her shaking hands in the air, showing her lack of weapons. "I will not hurt her or you. I promise."

Eyes fierce, Frederich raised the poker threateningly. "Talk fast. And don't make a move—I won't hesitate to use this."

Celine's heart broke a little—Frederich had never spoken harshly to her before. "It's the girl. Cherry, she's a shapeshifter Gunther and I brought back from Harvin. She made herself look like me and then did this with a potion." She waved a hand, showing her appearance. "You have to believe me, Frederich. I'm Celine." The words rushed out as she heard the thudding of the guards pounding down the corridor.

"Prove it then."

"How do you think I got in here?" Celine challenged him, desperation lacing her voice. "You know we're the only ones that know about the secret passage."

Frederich lowered his poker a few inches, just as the guards burst through the door.

"It's her." Eddie, a big burly guard, grabbed her by the arm.

"No, wait." Celine begged as she tried to shake off the iron vise gripping her arm. "Remember when you broke your arm? You told everyone you fell down the stairs? I know what really happened; you were in the stall with that horse after being told not to. I covered for you."

"Everyone knows what really happened." Frederich nodded at Eddie to take her away.

"And the time you broke mother's favourite vase? I told Father I did it so you wouldn't get punished." The words rushed out as the guards surrounded her. "She's not me," Celine insisted. "That's why Fifi didn't recognize her. Ask Sarah, she was there with me in Harvin; she knows what she can do."

"Wait." Frederich held up a hand to stop the guards.

"Your highness. Your father has ordered us to take her down to the dungeon. I can't go against his orders." Eddie's tone was firm, and his eyes were hard as he continued to wrestle Celine toward the door.

"She's going to take everything away from me. From us." Celine struggled and kicked, but the guards were ready this time, holding her so tight she knew she would have bruises. She glared as she spotted a familiar blonde head of hair coming into the room.

"You're not getting away with this." She hissed at Cherry, who cowered back against the wall. Cherry's face was frightened, but her eyes held an unmistakable gleam of triumph.

"That's enough. So sorry your highness." The guard bowed to Cherry as he hauled her away.

CELINE GLARED AT THE cold iron bars that surrounded her. Ignoring all her protests, the guards had unceremoniously deposited her in the cell, leaving her with just a bucket and a jug of water. Celine wrinkled her nose at the dank smell emanating from the pile of straw in the corner. Hugging her knees, she huddled in the corner to consider her options. If only the guards had been a bit slower, she might have swayed Frederich. The two siblings had always been close. There had to be some way of convincing him Cherry was a fraud.

Staring in a daze, she watched the small square of light march across the wall from the tiny prison window as the hours passed by. Eventually, a guard arrived bearing the standard prison fare, a fresh jug of water, a chunk of brown bread, and a bowl of soup. Knowing she had to keep up her strength, Celine swallowed her pride and choked down the bland fare. Leaving her empty bowl and cup at the door, she curled up in the hay, trying to avoid the prickly fibres that dug into the thin fabric of the nightgown she was still wearing.

A clatter of footsteps and rattle of keys woke Celine from her doze; she peered through the murky gloom, trying to find out who was there.

"Frederich?" A tiny ray of hope awakened as the familiar form came closer.

Frederich stopped by Celine's cell. "I've done some thinking, and I think—I think I believe you."

Celine's breath caught in her throat as Frederich searched her eyes. He paused, swallowing hard before he continued.

"But Father—King Erich isn't even willing to consider the idea. He just got Celine back. And she's good—that is, if you're right and she is Cherry. I'm not even sure what to think at this point." Frederich rubbed his face with his hands.

"Frederich. You came." Tears misted her eyes as Celine gripped the cold iron bars that separated them.

Frederich exhaled, "If you are Celine—and that's a big *if*—how can we make her change back to her original form. It's the only way to convince Father and Mother. They want to have a trial for you, and that's going to take some time."

"But we don't have time. Cherry's leaving in two weeks. Unless they delay her departure, we won't have a chance to prove who she really is."

"I know." Frederich shook his head. "And right now, she has them all convinced that you're an insane person who somehow managed to break into the castle."

"Well, I'll just have to work fast and get this done before she leaves then. I don't want to end up married to Prince Alexander." A tear rolled down Celine's cheek and dripped onto the stone floor.

Frederich crinkled his brow. "How do you know that's what she was planning?"

"I used the tunnel to watch the council meeting." Celine sniffed.

"Well, do you know what we can do to stop her?"

Celine had thought long and hard about this. "I think so. We have to get that collar back. When she was performing at the carnival, she had a metal collar around her neck. I think whoever was running the carnival used it to control her somehow. I opened it with a key that the fortune-teller gave me so I could bring her here with me."

"Do you know what happened to the collar and they key?"

Celine closed her eyes to think. "We were in one of the carnival tents when I took the collar off and I was in such a hurry, I left it there where I found her. I still have the key, though. It's in my jewellery box. That is, if she hasn't taken it by now."

Frederich leaned his head on the bars in frustration. "So to find the collar, we have to find the carnival and hope somehow they still have it and they'll give it to us?"

"It looks like it." Celine chewed on her lip. "Are you in?" She gave her brother a hopeful look as she stuck her hand through the bar, extending two fingers in the secret greeting they had invented as children.

Frederich returned the gesture. "I'm in. Let's get you out of here." He jingled the keys at his side.

"How did you get those?" Celine raised an eyebrow.

"You know where Father keeps extra sets of keys in his private office?" Frederich answered her question with one of his own.

"Behind the painting of Grandfather Bertie," Celine said with a grin as the iron lock clicked open. She stepped into the hallway.

"I asked Lucie to distract him after dinner. She got him to take her to the map room. You know how Father is once he starts talking about his maps." Celine rolled her eyes as Frederich closed and locked the door behind them, leading her up the narrow staircase. "You can't stay here, so Lucie and I got together a few things for you. You'll be safer out of the castle for the time being."

Celine glanced down the empty passageway. "Where is everyone?" she asked. The guard's station was abandoned. As much as Celine wanted her freedom, she hated to get any of the guards in trouble. After all, many of them had families of their own at home and they were only following orders. They had always been loyal to Celine and her family.

"I changed the rota. They haven't realized no one is here yet. But we have to hurry; they're going to be making their rounds soon." He hurried her down a narrow hall toward the door that led to a small courtyard. Only a storage area, really. Moonlight casted shadows across the small space, and Celine jumped as a rat scurried by, darting under an empty cask.

"I've got you a horse and some money. If you're careful, it should last you for a while." Celine followed Frederich as he strode across the courtyard toward the back of the stable.

"But what am I going to wear? I can't go like this." Celine gestured at her nightgown and bare feet.

"Lucie's getting clothes ready for you; she'll meet us in the stable. If you wear a hat and pull your hood up, no one will notice you've got no hair. I would have brought a wig, but I had so little time." Frederich opened a creaky wooden door at the side of the building. They entered the stables, the warm comforting smell of horses surrounding Celine reminded her of happier times. Only a small lantern lit the space occupied by rows of horses. A tabby cat emerged from the shadows to rub round Celine's ankles.

"Did you get my sword?" Celine's sword, her favourite possession, given to her on her sixteenth birthday—made to measure and perfectly weighted to fit her hand.

"I got the sword." Lucie rounded the corner, loaded with an armful of supplies. "I knew you wouldn't want to go anywhere without it." She gave Celine a sympathetic look, shaking her head in disapproval as she ran her eyes over Celine's bald head. "I can't believe that girl did this to you. It's a disgrace."

"What about Father and Mother? Are they still convinced Cherry is me?" Celine turned to Lucie as she waited anxiously for an answer.

Lucie nodded, her eyes sad. "She completely pulled the wool over their eyes. They wouldn't even listen when I told them they should at least come down and hear what you had to say. They're just so horrified that someone would go near their precious daughter that they can't even see the possibility of it."

Lucie handed a pile of clothes to Celine—a serviceable pair of fawn trousers, a linen tunic, and a hooded cape. "I didn't want you to have anything too noticeable," Lucie explained as Celine gratefully took the clothes, eager to shed her filthy nightgown.

"You get the horse saddled. I can help Celine," Lucie addressed Frederich, who obediently went to the tack room.

"I have a hat as well." Lucie waited as Celine stepped into the trousers. "And there's two extra sets of everything. I don't know how long this is going to take, and I don't want you to get caught out." She handed Celine a bulging leather satchel. "How is your face? Frederich told me you look completely different now?"

Celine grimaced. "I'm hideous, a completely different person."

"Can I see?" Lucie asked, her voice gentle.

Celine nodded, and Lucie held out her hand. A ball of golden flame appeared, casting a bright light over the two girls. Celine eyed the flames. Even after all this time, Lucie's magic never ceased to amaze her. Lucie reached out her other hand and stroked Celine's shorn head, her eyes swimming with unuttered thoughts.

"Do you think it will fade? Can you ask Lord Remy or Althea?" Celine bit her lip.

"I will." Lucie squeezed her hand.

"Take the side gate when you leave; the guards never look there. The key is in its usual spot," Frederich interrupted the girls as he led a brown horse toward the mounting block. "I'm putting you on Winston here because he's less noticeable than your horse."

Celine took the reins from her brother and led the horse to the mounting block.

"We'll do what we can from here," Frederich continued as he followed her, "I think a few of the council members aren't convinced Cherry is making a wise decision. Leave that with me; I'll talk to them. I've sent word to Gunther at his estate. If we get his testimony, it will make all the difference," Frederich promised as Celine swung into the saddle. Uncomfortable with goodbyes, he patted her on the leg. And that is how she left home. No fanfare, no crowds, just her brother and Lucie standing in the courtyard as she slipped away into the darkness; Celine knew the next few days would change everything.

"YOU DON'T HAVE ANY rooms?" Exhausted, Celine leaned over the wooden counter of the inn. After travelling all night, she was hoping to find a place to sleep for a few hours. But the only inn in the village of Bannard was full, and the next village was at least two hours away. Celine looked around, taking in her surroundings. The dining area, a large room dotted with wooden tables and smelling of soap and the remnants of breakfast—scrambled eggs and bacon—didn't *look* busy. Maybe they just didn't *want* to give her a room, she thought bitterly. Celine was used to her every whim being accommodated for sooner rather than later and was finding her new appearance had tangible drawbacks.

"Is there anywhere else I could stay?" Celine looked hopefully out the door at the scattering of houses clustered around the small market square. It didn't appear promising, but it never hurt to ask.

"Not really. Unless you want the stable." The innkeeper didn't seem too enthusiastic to even offer that.

"Fine." Celine took the offer. "And I also want lunch." She glanced hopefully at what she assumed was the kitchen door.

"Lunch isn't until noon." The innkeeper leaned back in his chair and clasped his hands over the spread of his stomach. "You can come back for it then, and it'll cost extra for oats if you're going to stable the horse." He jerked his chin toward Winston, who was dozing in the courtyard.

"Yes, that would be lovely." Celine turned to go.

"Wait. You haven't paid yet," the innkeeper called her back.

"Oh, of course." Flustered, Celine fished in her purse for the coins. After stabling Winston, she found a small cot in the corner of the stable and, covering herself with her cloak, lay down for some much needed rest.

After a nap and a wash with water from the well behind the stable, Celine's spirits improved. Keeping her distance from the other clients, she took a seat at one of the wooden tables, avoiding the few other travellers scattered around the room—travelling merchants and possibly a farmer or two. Hoping news of her escape hadn't spread, Celine kept her head down, her hat well pulled down.

"Here you are, dear." A short motherly woman, with grey hair pulled back in a bun placed a steaming mug of hot spiced coffee in front of her. Celine cupped the mug in her hands, enjoying the warmth before taking a sip of the bitter liquid. "You can add some milk if you like." The woman nudged a small blue pitcher toward Celine. "Looks like you've had a long day already. I'm Jean, so if you need anything, just give me a shout."

"Thank you; it's delicious." Celine wasn't sure she wanted to risk giving herself away, but she needed information, and this chatty woman seemed like a good place to start.

"Now, I've got the Ficandeau today. Would you like some of that, my dear?" Jean's round face creased in a smile.

"Yes, please." The smell of ham and bacon from the Ficandeau—a local stew—wafting from the kitchen, left Celine faint with hunger. She had devoured the dried meat Lucie had packed her in the first hour of her flight from the castle. Jean bustled away, deftly swiping a few plates from an empty table on her way back to the kitchen. Within moments, a large earthenware bowl of the savoury stew arrived, and a platter piled high with fresh bread. Celine dug in gratefully.

"So, what brings you to these parts?" Jean asked nosily as she set down another plate of bread in front of Celine. She eyed Celine's clothing, which was plain but clearly well-made and expensive.

"I'm just travelling." Celine shrank under Jean's suspicious gaze. "To Iasia."

"Hmm." Jean lingered. "Dangerous place, Iasia— full of magic. You have to be careful of everyone." She shivered.

"There's magic here too, isn't there?" Celine had always been curious to see what people really thought of the recent development of the ban on magic in Lovan being lifted.

"Yes." A grudging expression flashed across Jean's face. "We have nothing to do with it here in our town, though."

"Is that right?" Celine took advantage of the opportunity to gather information. "I hear there's a traveling carnival going through the towns—and they have mages for performers. Have you seen them?" She schooled her expression to look as innocent as possible.

"Oh, them." Jean sniffed. "Some people like that sort of thing. But I steer clear of all that nonsense. In my day, we put fortune-tellers where they belonged."

Celine's heart gave a thump of excitement. "When were they here? I heard they have some talented performers; I would love to get a look."

"Recently. Three, four weeks maybe. Nasty folk. I wouldn't trust them with a dog I didn't like." Jean's voice was icy.

"They can't *all* be bad." Taken aback that this seemingly pleasant woman could hold so much animosity toward complete strangers, Celine was at a loss for words.

"I wouldn't hedge my bets on that." Jean pursed her lips as she gathered plates.

"Do you know which way they were going?" Celine pressed as she dipped her bread in the stew in an attempt to look casual.

"As long as they're not here, I don't care where they went. All I heard is they took the road north—Iasia direction. Better if they stay with their own kind, anyway." Jean turned, balancing a stack of plates, leaving Celine to her thoughts.

Scooping up another bit of stew with her bread, she chewed thoughtfully. It could be the same carnival—after all, there couldn't be that many in the area and they would need to travel slowly, staying for at least few days in each town before moving on to the next. Decision made, she pushed her chair back.

After Celine had paid her bill to the sullen innkeeper, she mounted Winston, heading north toward Iasia.

THIS IS IT, thought Celine as she rode into Illes, just across the border from Iasia. Several valuable days had passed while Celine searched for the carnival. She nearly cried with happiness when she spotted the familiar tents pitched in the market square. The performers were out, surrounded by the usual crowd as they went through their routines.

After leaving Winston at the inn, she walked down the main street toward the square. Now came the real challenge, to get the collar. She patted the sword strapped her side. A precaution only, she convinced herself when she buckled in on earlier. Celine stopped in the town of Avender and bought a paper wrapped packet of sugar roasted nuts. For once grateful for the unwanted disguise, she melted into the crowd, edging her way toward the tents. Her best chance would be to find and take the collar while the performers and Karl were otherwise occupied. Drawing the hood of her cloak over her head, she slipped behind a stall selling skewers of spiced, roasted meat, its rich salty scent filling the air in thin lines of blue smoke. From there, it was a few steps across to the fabric merchant, its stall lined with swathes of colourful fabrics, making it an excellent place to blend in. She ducked behind a pair of women fingering bolts of colourful dyed cotton before moving on, skulking closer and closer to the pitched tents.

Celine stood up and glanced around, making sure there was no one near the tents before casually strolling in their direction, forcing herself to amble enough to not look suspicious to bystanders. When she reached them, her heart was pounding, and her mouth was dry. She checked one last to time to make sure no one was nearby before she ducked under the frayed flap of the largest tent, taking a moment to let her eyes adjust to the dimly lit interior. A row of beds lined up inside the tent told her there must be several occupants. She moved efficiently toward a large canvas bag that seemed the most likely place to hold a valuable item. Digging through, she found nothing but clothes—a few worn dresses and shabby tunics. She moved her attention to the mattresses, feeling underneath with her hand. Still nothing. She sat back on her heels. She would have to move fast if she didn't want to get caught. The likelihood of a valuable item being left in such an accessible place seemed improbable, almost bordering on ridiculous. But she had to try.

After sneaking into two more tents and finding nothing, discouragement gripped Celine. Not only did she not find the collar, there were no items of value anywhere. She scratched her head, wondering where they would keep them. Karl was too clever to leave something like that unguarded. She stood up, rubbing the ache in the small of her back. She slid out of the tent, and then, across the square, a colourful sign caught her eye. *Of course, the fortune-teller.* Gerta did all her work in the tent and could easily keep any eye on any valuables. Now, she only had to figure out a way to get in.

I'll have to create a distraction, Celine thought as she crept around the back of the tent she had been in and re-joined the bustling marketplace, sidling up to a throng of people gathered around the fire dancers. Finding a wooden bench, she sat down to think. Tendrils of smoke from the roasted meat drifted into in her eyes and she waved it away with her hand. *That's it.* Her hand froze and her heart gave a thump of excitement. *I can smoke her out. Then I'll get the collar and make a run for it.* This plan *had* to work. She would make sure it did. She only had a little more than a week left before Cherry went back to Iasia. Cherry would push for a brief engagement and once they completed the marriage ceremony, it would be impossible to back out of it.

It's time for a distraction, thought Celine as she tied Winston next to a dappled mare at the railing in front of the town square. "I might have to leave in a hurry," she explained to the horse. She tossed a coin to the boy in the tattered brown coat who was standing nearby. He jumped to attention.

"Can you look after my horse for me?" Celine spoke kindly. "I can give you another coin when I get back."

"Of course, miss." The boy's face lit up with eagerness. Winston whickered, nosing the boy's hand for treats with his velvety nostrils.

Celine slung a cloth bag of supplies over her shoulder and strolled past the rows of venders toward the fortune-teller's tent. Out of the corner of her eye, she saw Karl standing with a trio of acrobats. He was wearing his green velvet jacket and had a small bag slung across his chest. Celine hoped that it didn't contain the collar, but she would have to think about that later. Turning her head, she carried on, waiting for a pretty brunette girl to enter the tent before tiptoeing around the back of the tent. Voices murmured in the tent, the girl's high and clear in contrast to the smoky tones of the fortune-teller. Heart in her mouth, she took her supplies out of the satchel she carried— a pile of damp rags she had taken from the kitchen garden back at the inn, her flint, and a bit of tinder. Sparking her flint, she lit the rags, their dampness creating a cloud of choking smoke. Hoping she wouldn't cause too much damage, she set it behind the tent, lifting the side wall a few inches to draw the smoke inside. *That should do it.* She slid around to the side of the tent, crouching down to wait. Moments later, her efforts were rewarded.

"Fire," a voice shouted. "The fortune-teller's tent is on fire." Celine forced herself to stand still as the girl and the fortune teller emerged, coughing and spluttering from the doorway. Knowing she had mere seconds to act, she lifted the side of the tent and wriggled through. Blinking her eyes against the stinging smoke, she peered through the gloom, searching for storage. After turning over several of the colourful cushions, and rummaging through a chest of drawers, her eyes settled on the small table with the crystal ball, a round shape underneath its black velvet covering. Of course, she lifted the tablecloth. It wasn't a table at all. Underneath was a wooden trunk, exquisitely carved with finely crafted brass fittings. Fingers shaking, Celine snatched off the cloth, sending the crystal ball tumbling to the ground, and opened the trunk, rifling through the contents. There were heavy bags of coins, a small pouch with a green stone necklace, and a silver backed mirror, its handle worn with use. She lifted an ancient-looking book, the writing on the cover faded with age. And there it was. Underneath the book was the collar, gleaming up at her.

Celine's heart pounded with excitement as she lifted the collar and slid it into her bag. Then, eyes watering from the smoke, she turned to go, being careful to keep her sword out of the way as she squirmed back under the side of the tent.

"Not so fast." A rough hand grabbed the back of Celine's cloak, stopping her short with a cry of surprise. "You're not going to get away with this." It was Karl, with Gerta standing behind him.

Celine struggled and kicked, fighting to slip out of the cloak, but he held tight. He wrapped his other arm around her torso before she could reach her sword. "Gerta." He nodded toward the dark-eyed woman who took the sword out of its sheath.

"I think you might have something of mine." His hot sour breath washed over her, and she cringed against his iron grip.

"You must be mistaken. I don't have anything of yours," Celine protested, still breathing hard from her effort.

"You won't mind if we just take a look then." He smirked. Celine's shoulders sagged. There would be no chance to escape if he found the stolen collar.

Gerta took the bag from Celine's neck, rooting through it and pulling out the collar, the strange symbols on it glinting in the light. The look on her face was almost apologetic as she handed the collar over to Karl, who slid it into the deep pocket of his jacket.

Karl's grip around Celine tightened until she could hardly breathe. "I don't think you know exactly what you've done, sweetheart. That collar was the only thing keeping that—*thing* from wreaking havoc."

"You mean Cherry?"

"Oh, is that what she's calling herself now?" Karl sneered. In one swift motion, he twisted her arm behind her back, steering her towards the fortune-teller's tent. The smoke had cleared thanks to a bucket of water poured over it by one of the carnival workers, and only a wet pile of charred rags and a lingering odour remained to show what had happened there.

"Wait. What are you going to do with me?" Celine dragged her feet, trying to slow their progress.

"You know what the penalty for thieves is." Karl yanked her through the opening of the tent, wrenching her arm until she cried out in pain.

"No, you can't do that to me." Celine's voice pitched high with fear. The last thing she needed was to be forced back to the castle for a trial. "Please, just let me go. I have money, I can pay you whatever you want."

Karl laughed, a hoarse bark. "We weren't going to have a trial. Too much hassle. We'll just take care of this ourselves, the old-fashioned way."

"What do you mean the old-fashioned way?" Celine trembled.

Karl ignored her. "Gerta?" He nodded toward the fortune-teller who drew the hood back and took Celine's hat off her head, revealing jagged tufts of hair. "I see she got to you." He gave Celine a little shove, and she half sat, half fell onto the hard ground. Grabbing a piece of cord, he securely tied her hands and legs together with a series of thick knots.

"Now, here's what we'll do." Karl sat back on his heels. "You are going to get her back for us. And then I'll help you fix this little problem." He flicked her shorn head. "And, on top of that, I'm going to need a few favours thrown in. After all, I'm the only one here right now who knows who you are." He flashed a toothy grin.

"But I can't get to her," Celine protested. "That's why I needed the collar. I can't go back without it, unless I want to end up in the dungeon." She twisted her wrists against bite of the cord wrapped around them.

"Hmm..." Karl scratched his chin. "She's getting better at this. I have to admit she's smarter than I thought she was. Well, I'm afraid you're stuck then; we'll have the trial." He sat on a tasselled cushion and leaned back, crossing his legs in front of him.

"Are you sure there's nothing else I can do for you?" She threw Gerta a pleading look, knowing that she would be easier to convince than Karl.

"What is it you think you can do for us?" Karl scoffed before Gerta could answer. "I mean, your family walks around like they're some kind of saviours to the mages but lifting the ban on magic did nothing to help anyone. People don't change their opinions overnight. You think you can undo hundreds of years of damage with just one tiny policy change?"

"Wait, you have magic too?" Temporarily distracted, Celine wondered what kind of magic Karl might have running through his veins.

Karl remained silent, ignoring her question.

"You could start by offering protection to those who have magic. Restitution if there are crimes committed against them," Gerta spoke up, her raspy voice low.

"But surely that's in place already." Celine's voice was shocked. "I mean, according to the law, and the guild, you have every right that any other citizen has."

Karl sneered. "Any citizens? Ha! Are all your citizens chased from pillar to post, sneered at in every town? They might come to see the performance, even give us a coin or two—but they would never let us in. Do you think people *like* living like this?" he waved his hand at the shabby canvas walls of the tent. He glared at Celine.

Celine stared at the floor, discomfort forgotten. She had an inkling of course that things weren't well with the mage community. She remembered the unforgiving, judgemental comments of the woman at the inn. But she hadn't realized things were this bad.

Karl stood, smoothing down the frayed edges of his velvet jacket. "Well, that's enough talk about politics for one day. You keep the little princess in here. I've got to get back out there and make sure everyone's behaving themselves." Without another glance at Celine, he left, the flap of the tent swishing into place behind him.

Celine watched his shadow disappear around the side of the tent. She sneaked a glance at Gerta, who sat still as a stone at her small table, hands folded in front of her.

"Why did you want me to free her if she was going to cause so much trouble?" Celine asked. "I don't understand why you gave me the key."

"The story is just beginning." Gerta's deep voice was calm.

Celine waited for her to continue. "Story? What do you mean story?" she asked after a long pause when Gerta remained silent.

"Yes, and your choices are going to make our story. You made your choices and Cherry made hers." Celine bit her lip, thinking about the cryptic words as Gerta tidied the mess she had made in the tent, replacing the crystal ball on the trunk and covering it with the velvet cloth. Reaching into the pocket of her patchwork skirt, she pulled out a small bone-handled knife. Celine tensed, eyeing the glinting metal blade nervously. Gerta moved toward Celine, kneeling beside her as she pressed herself back against the floor.

"You chose kindness, so kindness will be returned to you. Besides, we need your help." Gerta cut through the cords around Celine's wrists. Celine stretched out her fingers, embracing the sharp nip of the blood flowing back into her veins.

"Now, hurry, he'll be back soon." Gerta made a shooing motion with her hands.

Celine paused at the opening of the tent. "But what about you? Won't he be angry when he knows you let me go?" A worried expression flashed through her eyes.

"Let me worry about Karl. Just remember us when you're free. Come back for us; they deserve better." Gerta gestured toward the other tents as she pierced Celine with her dark, knowing eyes. "He's got the others under his thumb as well, and you must be careful, he's more dangerous than you can imagine. Karl is a collector."

Celine raised questioning eyes to Gerta's. Collector wasn't a term she was familiar with. "He collects talent. Finds people who have abilities and uses them to make money. Travels around from place to place looking. He's always looking for more. And when they're not useful anymore, he sells them to the highest bidder." Gerta spit the words out with disgust.

Celine reeled. "But *how*. Doesn't the mage guild protect them?"

"The guild?" Gerta's voice grew hard. "Most people can't afford the fees. And even if they could, the guild is so green, they're not established enough to do much of anything at all. They need help—we need help."

"What can I do? I'm running myself." Celine gestured toward her outfit, streaked with dirt and reeking of smoke.

"He leaves the valuables—the money—in the tent with me, but he controls us with a medallion he keeps on his person. Find a way to take it away from him, then bring it to me. And you have to hurry. Karl is only here to make another collection, then he's heading back to Corvan. There's something big happening there soon; he hasn't said, but I can see it coming. We have to get away before then or many people are going to be sold. Now go, I'll keep watch for you; you have a few minutes to get away." With one last glance at the mysterious woman, Celine was away.

Celine scurried out of the tent, slinking through the crowd. *Now how am I going to get that medallion from him,* she thought, frustration building as she stopped behind a display of carved wooden furniture. She paused, pretending to examine a chest of drawers. "Can I help you?" The vendor, a wiry man with a shock of spiky red hair, hovered nearby. He eyeballed the fine cloth of Celine's cloak, hoping for a sale.

"Just browsing." Celine ran a finger along the smooth wood, combing the area for a glimpse of Karl's distinctive green jacket.

"We have that in mahogany as well," the man suggested, as Celine lingered, wondering how much longer she could keep the merchant at bay. Her eyes scanned the marketplace. There, only two stalls away, she spotted Karl, speaking to one of the acrobats. Quickly, she knelt down, pretending to examine a drawer and trying to keep out of sight, but she was too late. Karl was staring straight at her.

"Thief!" Karl roared as he pointed a finger at Celine. The blood drained from Celine's face. She turned to the furniture vender, who was staring at her in shock.

Celine couldn't get caught again; it would be a disaster. Whirling around, she scrambled away, knocking over a rack and scattering a stack of wooden trays in her panic. Recovering quickly from his surprise, the vender reached out his arm to grab her, but desperation gave her speed and she ducked under it just in time, rolling to the ground before springing back up to her feet again. With Karl in hot pursuit, she sprinted away, arms pumping as she pelted through the square, shoving people out of the way in her haste. Weaving her way through the stalls, she dashed back into the fabric merchant's stall, squatting down behind the bolts of dyed canvas. Spotting an opening at the back of the stall, she slipped out, tagging along with a group of farmers heading toward the inn.

WHEN CELINE ARRIVED back at the inn, she found the innkeeper who agreed to give her a recently vacated room. Sinking down on her the narrow bed, Celine planned her next move. Finding the medallion and moving a large group of people would be no easy feat. But Celine knew if she left them there, Karl would find a way to cause them trouble. Celine took out her satchel, finding some clean clothes and changing her heavy woolen cloak for a light one. It would do for now to disguise her. At least long enough to let her go back for Winston. She searched through her bag, looking for something—anything—she could use to help. She paused when her hand settled on a familiar leather case—something given to all the guards as part of their standard equipment. *The practical Lucie must have included it*, she thought gratefully as her fingers fumbled with the leather ties. The case opened to reveal a stash of medical supplies, a neat roll of bandages, a few implements and a collection of glass bottles and vials, their contents neatly labelled with bits of paper. She found the one she was looking for and put it in her pocket, hoping it would be enough to accomplish her goal.

Celine examined herself in the mirror that hung on the wall. She took off her hat, turning her head back and forth, looking critically at her shorn head. A pang of anger and regret shot through her as she remembered the golden waves of hair she used to take for granted. Narrowing her eyes, she leaned closer. Was it... getting longer? She took a piece between two fingers. She was certain it was at least an inch or even two inches longer than when it was first cut. Running her fingers through it, she gave it a thoughtful tug. She opened the curtains, then returned to the mirror, turning her face from side to side. The blotches had faded, bringing her skin back to its former porcelain smoothness, and her eyelashes seemed to grow back as well.

Spirits bolstered by her new discovery, Celine covered herself with her cloak and went back to the market, forcing herself to dawdle. Her sword hung at her side and this time, as an extra precaution, she had tucked a dagger in her boot, its solid length providing her with an extra sense of security. Eyes alert, she headed for the spot where she had left Winston.

"Would you like to earn even more coins?" she asked the ragged-looking boy as she untied the horse. His eyes lit up, giving her the answer she was hoping for.

"There's a man in a green velvet jacket. He's with the performers, and I want you to follow him. Do you think you can do it without letting him see you? I'll give you one silver now, and another when you come back. You can find me tonight at the Illes Cross Inn and tell me everything you saw." She handed him a coin, which he quickly snatched from her hand and pushed into his pocket with a cheeky grin.

"All right, miss." He scampered off.

Celine took Winston and put him in the stable, giving him an extra ration of oats to thank him for his patience. She left him nose down, munching happily, and went to her room to wait.

Opting to have food sent to her room, Celine was lying on the bed, feet propped up on a cushion, when there was a rap at the door.

"I did what you asked, miss." The boy came in, peering around at the simple room with curious eyes. "Say, is that a dagger?" He touched the weapon on the bed beside Celine with reverence. "I've never seen one up close before."

"You haven't?" Celine sat up, surprised. When growing up at the castle, weapons had been a part of everyday life.

"No, miss. My family is—was farmers. Except my cousin. He went away to be a soldier." A note of pride crept into the boy's voice and his green eyes shone, lighting up his thin face.

"And what does your family do now?"

The light left the boy's eyes, his face drooped. "They got the fever, so they couldn't keep the farm anymore—it's just me now."

Celine's heart broke for the boy, and the words spilled out her mouth before she could take them back. "I need a stable boy. Do you want to come work for me?"

"Really, miss?"

"Of course." Celine's voice held a confidence she didn't feel. A tagalong boy was hardly going to be an asset. But she couldn't leave him on his own either. "I'm not going home right away though, but you can come with me. I'll let you take care of Winston."

"He's a lovely horse, he is." Admiration coloured the boy's voice.

"Right, so that's settled." Celine stood up, brushing off her hands while secretly wondering what she was going to do with this adorable waif while completing her mission. "Now, if you're going to work for me, I need to know what your name is."

"You can call me Tommy," the boy's voice was cheerful.

"Well, Tommy, we have another job to do."

Tommy had done a surprisingly good job of following Karl, his small stature letting him blend in with the crowd and remain unseen. Unfortunately for Celine, Karl was a man of few vices. When he wasn't organizing the members of the carnival, he preferred to keep to himself. Never once had Tommy seen him set foot in a tavern.

"If we could just get to his food or drink, everything will be good," Celine moaned, flopping back on the lumpy pillow.

"Oh, I can do that." Tommy spoke confidently.

"You can? How?" Celine sat up, her face brightening.

"He likes the mead at one of the stalls. The one nearest the fountain."

"Do you think you could slip something in his drink?"

"Probably." Tommy fingered the material of his new breeches. Celine had sent a few coins with him when he went to the market to replace the rags he was wearing. "If I wear my old clothes, no one even notices me. I just blend in with the others." He referred to the group of ragged children that gathered at the market every morning. "If I give them a few coins, I could get some of them to distract him for me."

"That would be perfect." Celine's eyes sparkled with excitement. "Do you think he'll go there tonight?"

CELINE SLIPPED DOWN the back stairs of the Illes Cross, cringing as a loose floorboard creaked under her foot. Luckily, there was so much coming and going in the inn that the sound didn't even register, and she slipped out the back door unnoticed. Tommy had returned thirty minutes earlier, revealing to her that after a long wait, Karl had stopped by the stall for a tankard of mead, and just as Tommy had promised, his friends had distracted Karl just long enough for Tommy to slip the potion in his drink.

"I hope it works." Celine joined Tommy near the cluster of tents as agreed beforehand. "I only have the one dose, and I don't think the apothecary is open anymore." Despite the late hour, the market was still bustling. Celine watched as Karl's acrobats somersaulted to a cheering crowd across the ground near the fountain. Safe under the cover of darkness, Celine felt confident the noise of the market was enough to cover noise she and Tommy might make. Approaching the tents, they began searching for Karl. He was in the third tent, stretched out on a small cot with his mouth hanging open as he snored loudly. Celine gestured with her finger for Tommy to come.

"You stand guard; I'll go in and get what I need," she whispered. "If someone comes, shout."

She tiptoed inside, wrinkling her nose against the stench of stale sweat. When Karl murmured in his sleep, his leg jerking, Celine's heart nearly stopped in her mouth, but he rolled over and settled back to sleep.

Inching forward, she moved the front of his shirt back with a finger and saw it—a heavy gold medallion gleaming against the swarthy skin. She touched it, recoiling at the ominous feeling emitting from the dull metal. Sliding her finger under the medallion, she eased it up, searching for a clasp. After some manoeuvring, she slid it around and with trembling fingers, opened the clasp, gathering the medallion into her hands. An unpleasant buzzing sensation surged through her hand and up her arm when she touched the object. Magic, she recognized the feeling from the few magical objects King Erich and Queen Isabella had recovered when they lifted the ban. She wrapped the medallion in a scrap of cloth and buried it in the bottom of her satchel before she turned to the unpleasant job of searching his pockets for the collar—only lint and a few small coins. He must have put the collar somewhere, but where? Her eyes roamed the interior of the tent. Aside from some clothes and a few cooking utensils, it contained very little. She rifled through the scattered belongings, desperate fingers quivering with nerves.

"Hurry," Tommy hissed, interrupting her frantic search. "Someone's coming." Celine's heart plunged as she turned to leave.

"Did you get it?" Tommy's eyes gleamed with excitement as she opened her satchel to reveal the medallion. "That must be worth some money, miss," he breathed in awe, looking closely at the strange inscription running around the outside of the flat round object.

"I found the medallion, but I didn't find the collar. That's what I really need. Maybe Gerta knows where he keeps it." Celine knew she had mere minutes to act as she dashed toward the fortune-teller's tent. "She'll know what to do with this too." She shuddered; even in her satchel, she could feel the strange power of the medallion radiating.

Celine burst into Gerta's tent, interrupting her session with a portly woman hiding under a large purple scarf. The woman whipped her head around, alarmed at Celine's sudden entrance, then relaxed, realizing it was a stranger.

"Excuse me," Celine murmured, ducking her head to go back outside.

"No, that's quite all right, my dear. We were just finished here." Gerta gave the woman a kind smile, watching as she wrapped the scarf around her head, presumably so no one would recognize her.

"Many people still don't approve of us here," Gerta explained as she straightened the velvet cloth covering her trunk. "I take it you were successful?"

"I found the medallion, but I couldn't find the collar anywhere." Celine's troubled eyes met Gerta's deep brown pools.

"He must have it hidden." Gerta was unruffled. "All in its own time."

Celine clenched her teeth but remained silent. She didn't *have* time. "What should I do with it?" she asked the other woman, shifting her feet in the scatter of grit and sand that still covered the floor of the tent.

"Bring it here." Gerta took a pair of tongs and put a few lumps of charcoal into her copper brazier. They flared, casting a red glow across her face.

Celine took the medallion out of her satchel, being careful not to touch it. The symbols scrolling around the outer edge of the medallion seemed to shift and move in the dim light. She held it out.

Wrapping her hand in a cloth, Gerta took the medallion, muttering a few words under her breath as she dropped it on the hot coals. Billows of thick choking smoke rolled out of the brazier, filling the tent with an acrid, bitter smell. Celine coughed, eyes watering. Gerta waited, keeping a watchful eye on the fire, and when the smoke cleared, Celine felt as if a weight had lifted off her chest. Her thoughts were suddenly clearer.

"Was that it?" She lifted her eyes to Gerta's.

"That was it." Gerta waved away a few lingering tendrils of smoke. "Now, they should have felt that too, but we may need to explain it to them. And we'll have to get away from Karl; I can guarantee that's not the only trick he has up his sleeves. How much time do you think we have until he wakes up?"

"Maybe a few hours?"

"That will have to do. If we can make it to the Iasian border before he catches up to us, King Ruben and Queen Abigail's men will protect us."

"But what about the collar?" Celine's voice was anxious. "I have to get it back."

"If it's not on his person, I don't know where it is. But we can look for it when we pack up. We're used to moving around a lot, so we should be ready to leave in an hour. Meet us back here then."

Dismissed, Celine found herself standing outside the tent, bewildered at the speed with which Gerta had taken control.

"What happened?" Tommy's eager face popped around the corner of the tent.

"Let's get Winston. We're going to Iasia."

CHAPTER SEVEN

There were thirty-three of them. Celine counted. Twice. Thirty-five if she counted herself and Tommy. Thirty-three people she was now responsible for. The rag-tag group comprising the acrobat troupe, a trick magician and his assistant—who turned out to be his daughter—Gerta, and a collection of others. All had some sort of magical skill or ability.

"Are you all ready?" The afternoon sun was quickly fading, the square only occupied by a few merchants still packing up their wares for the night. Karl's tent stood at the end of the square, a lone triangle surrounded by bare ground.

Gerta sat at the front of the group, perched on a white mule with a belled harness. Her bracelets jingled as she lifted her arm, signalling for them to begin the journey.

Celine and Gerta led the group down the main street, the jingling harnesses causing more than a few noses to press up against their windows as they passed. Tommy, who had opted not to ride in the wagon, sat proudly in front of her, reaching down occasionally to stroke Winston's coat.

It was slow going. Several of the younger ones were flagging after a long day of work. When Celine saw more than a few pairs of drooping eyes, she let Winston drift to the rear of the party.

"Do you think they can keep up the pace?" Celine asked Brainard in a low voice—he seemed to be the leader of the group. Older than the rest of them, he was a burly man with wiry brown hair sticking out from under his cap. He was accompanied by his daughter Miranda, a quiet girl who remained glued to his side, barely speaking a word.

"We need to go a little farther to make sure Karl can't catch up with us. Do you think they can do it?" Celine lowered her voice. Most of the group were young and, although willing, seemed a bit confused by the unexpected turn of events. "I want to be across the border by morning; I don't what else Karl is capable of."

"Aye." Brainard nodded in agreement. "I think Karl's promised a few of them to specific buyers, and they aren't the type you want to offend, if you catch my drift." He shifted wary eyes to Miranda, who gave him a wan smile before lowering her eyes. "I overheard him talking to one of his messengers. He could be a bit careless at times; we knew more than he thinks we do. See Miranda here, she's a sizer, and I know that's in demand among the thieves." He gave his daughter a protective look.

"A sizer?" Celine gave Brainard a questioning look.

"She can change her size. Handy if you want to lift a bit of jewellery. Rare too." A note of pride entered his voice.

Celine pressed her lips together, trying not to think about what the intentions of the other buyers might be.

"And how did no one notice he was doing this?" Celine had wondered this for a while. "Why *can't* the guild protect their interests?"

"The guild?" Brainard chuckled. "Karl is *in* the guild. If it were his word against ours, he would come out on top."

Celine drew her lip into her teeth, worrying it as she thought for a moment. "What about the king's guards then? Couldn't they have helped you? I know King Erich would never allow this had he known about it."

"The medallion put a silencing ward on us. Some tried, but the words came out gibberish. The only one who knew their way around Karl was Gerta." Brainard cast an admiring glance toward head of the line where Gerta swayed on her mule.

"Where would he even get something that powerful anyway?" Celine shuddered as her mind drifted back to the thick oily aura seeping from the medallion.

"One of his friends made it for him. It cost him a pretty penny, I'd say. Things like that don't come cheap. He's going to be out for blood when he finds it missing."

"Do you know where he might have got the collar? You know the one that Cherry was wearing?"

"Probably the same person." Brainard clucked at his horse. "He never let us see who it was, but from what I do know, it was someone powerful—influential. But when we get to Iasia, that won't matter as much. King Ruben and Queen Abigail have no tolerance for this, and they have a strong guild that can deal with him."

Celine realized at the pace they were going, they were at least an hour from the border. The sky was lightening from black to grey and a line of pink peeked through the trees on the eastern horizon.

"We'll still have to get to King Ruben's men, even after we cross the border. After we reach Iasia, we can go off the main road and find a quiet place to camp so everyone can get a rest." Celine noticed Miranda's head was nodding. And she wasn't the only one; the group was exhausted and wouldn't be able to keep going much longer.

Finally, they reached the border. Here, instead of thick forest, the trees were spaced out with large rocks, granite. Celine recognized a large boulder protruding into their path. This area was known for sheep; Celine spotted a few grey shapes huddled together as they slept. Presently, they came to a path—nothing more than a track, really. But it led off the main road, offering safety. "This way." She guided Winston to the front of the group, leading the way down the path. The three wagons creaked, rocking over the rough ground as the sturdy mules pulled them steadily over the rutted trail.

Celine leaned in to whisper to Gerta. "They can't go too much farther without a rest; we can stop here and regroup."

Gerta nodded, the fine lines around her eyes showing her fatigue. "I think there's a lake up ahead; it's near a hunting lodge, but that's rarely used. I camped here often when I was a child."

Sure enough, around the bend, a lake appeared, the surface of it glittering in the rising sun.

"We'll stop here." Celine turned to the group, speaking in her most commanding voice. They turned off the road and headed for a strand of beach. An opening in the trees gave them access to a pebbly beach covered in small granite stones. The group lost no time pitching their tents and soon had set up a tidy campsite complete with a blazing fire.

"Have some porridge." Fiona, an acrobat, pushed back her mane of fiery red curls as she ladled Celine a steaming bowl of porridge. She sprinkled a crumbling layer of brown sugar on top. "There's one for Tommy as well."

Celine took the bowl gratefully, settling on a flat rock and breathing in the sugary scented steam rising from the bowl. Fiona settled next to her, tipping her face up to the sunshine.

"We can't thank you enough for what you did." Fiona blew on a spoonful of porridge before putting it into her mouth.

"Well, I couldn't live with myself if I had left you there." Celine kicked a pile of damp leaves with her boot. "How did you come to be with him, anyway?"

"My mother and father passed away in the riots," Fiona answered. "The people in town forced me out of my home and didn't have anywhere to go. He offered shelter. He seemed kind—at first—and I didn't think I had any other options. Well, not ones I wanted to consider." Her long lashes fanned her cheek. "When I told him I was a dancer, he put me with the acrobats. It wasn't all bad; I had the other acrobats. We were all in it together. It's when people started disappearing, we all knew he was behind it. And then he showed us the medallion. If any of us touched it, we would die."

"I still don't understand how he gets away with it." Celine scooted over on her rock when Alanna, Fiona's acrobatic partner, came to join them.

"He keeps quiet, moves around a lot, and uses coin when nothing else works." Allana pitched into the conversation as she settled herself, twisting her flexible legs and tucking them underneath her.

"And the medallion, how did that work?"

"With this." Fiona set down her bowl. Drawing up her sleeve, she held out her arm to Celine, revealing a tattoo etched in the pale delicate skin of her inner elbow. Celine peered down, squinting at the strange script running across the pale skin of her arm. The text matched the script carved into the edge of the medallion.

"He did this to you?" Gently, Celine took Fiona's arm. "How does it work?"

"Magic," Fiona replied. "Dark magic. It's not his, but he has access; he has some very powerful friends."

"Well, when I get back home, there will be no more of this." Celine set her chin stubbornly.

"When you get back?" Alanna questioned.

"Back to the castle. I only came to find Karl to get Cherry's collar back. I don't actually look like this." Celine gestured to her face and hair, which had grown another inch overnight.

"Cherry did *that* to you?" Fiona's eyes widened. "She was always so shy and quiet; I didn't think she would be capable of that."

"Well, she's not shy anymore." Celine scraped the last of her porridge from the bottom of the bowl. "But I intend to take my rightful place back, and when I do, I'm going to track down Karl and every single one of his friends." Her expression was steel.

Leaving Fiona and Allana by the fire, Celine took her bowl and spoon to the lake to wash them. It was while scrubbing them with a handful of clean sand and rinsing it in the icy clear water, she heard a shuffling noise behind her. "Do you want me to do yours too—oh!"

Turning around, she realized in shock she wasn't talking to one of the performers, but a huge shaggy bear. The bear stood on his back feet, sniffing the air before dropping back down and running straight for her. Dropping her bowl in the lake, she reached for her sword. Sliding it out of the scabbard, she swung it up, nicking him in the shoulder and ducking under the giant paw that swiped through the air. Rolling away, she sprung up on her feet as the bear roared in frustration, beady eyes glittering in anger and pain. Again, the heavy paw swept down, catching the corner of her cloak. Celine stumbled back, tripping over one of the sharp rocks that littered the beach.

"Go away!" Celine shouted, voice hoarse with desperation. But it was too late for that; the bear was furious, throwing its head back in another mighty roar. Knowing this was her only chance, she thrusted herself forward, burying her sword in the bear's chest. In one swift move, she pulled it back out with a nightmarish sucking sound. The bear grunted, dropping to all fours, but continued to press towards her, rearing forward on clumsy feet.

Celine shouted again. Members of the carnival ran to the lake, but unarmed, they were helpless to do anything but watch. Tommy, however, undeterred by his lack of weapons, grabbed a long branch. Shouting loudly, he waved it at the bear. The large animal swung its head around, focusing cold marble eyes on the small boy.

"No, Tommy!" shouted Celine. Desperately, she swung again, this time catching the bear in the neck as he turned toward Tommy. "Get back." The bear reeled at the hit but continued to lurch toward Tommy, snorting through blood and pain.

Gritting her teeth, Celine lunged forward again, burying the sword to the hilt in the bear's chest. With a thud, the bear fell to the ground; the tremor shivered the leaves in the nearby trees. Then all was still.

With a sob, Celine drew out her sword and dropped it to the ground, reaching for the small boy. "You idiot." She wiped a tear from her cheek. "What were you thinking, going after him with a stick like that?" She wrapped him in her arms, and he squeaked in surprise. "Never do that again."

"I couldn't let him get you," Tommy argued, squirming from her tight embrace. "Not after all you've done for me." Despite his protest, Celine gave him another tight squeeze before picking up her sword, rinsing it in the lake and wiping it carefully on the edge of her cloak. Rising to her feet, she saw the members of the carnival had silently gathered around her. Wordlessly, Gerta stepped forward and put her arm around Celine, leading her back to the campsite.

CHAPTER EIGHT

Celine sat on a log by the lake watching Tommy. He had fashioned a fishing pole from a piece of wire and a stick and was busy flinging it into the water.

"I'll catch us a fish for dinner." He grinned over his shoulder at Celine as he flung the wire again, nearly losing his bait in the process.

Celine smiled at the boy before turning back to Gerta and Brainard. The three of them had become the unofficial leaders of the group and were in the midst of discussing their next move.

"Everyone's tired." Brainard combed his fingers through his beard. "And we're far enough off the path that we should be safe for the time being. What do you think, Gerta?"

Gerta closed her eyes, her face still in concentration. "I don't sense any immediate danger. But that doesn't mean things can't change." She sighed. "I'd feel better if we were in safe hands, of course. But I think you're right. They need to rest." Her skirt flapped in the breeze as she stretched her legs out on a rock.

Celine nodded in agreement, eyes on the flickering water. As anxious as she was to restore appearance and regain her rightful place, she knew she had to get the group to safety first.

"I got one." Jumping up and down in excitement, Tommy held up his line, a silver fish wriggling at the end.

"Well done." Celine waved at him.

"I'm going to catch another." Grinning, Tommy put his fish safely in a bucket he'd wrangled from the one of the performers and baited his hook again, tossing the line back into the lake.

Leaving Gerta and Brainard to their discussion, Celine wandered along the edge of the lake, skirting the area where she had killed the bear. Arlo and Cathal, two burly twins, had taken on the onerous task of skinning the bear, taking the meat and setting it aside for roasting over the fire. As she passed, she could see them parcelling out the portions and tossing the entrails to the dogs, who were wolfing up the scraps.

Sticking to the shore, she picked her way through a marshy patch, the thick sticky mud sucking at her boots. The terrain here was so different from what she was used to in Lovan. The steep hills were covered with scrubby grass and hardy trees instead of the lush woods and rich farmland she was used to seeing. She climbed over a boulder, the rough surface of the granite biting into her hands. The campsite had long disappeared around the corner of the shore, and she relished the quiet solace, only interrupted by gentle waves and twittering birds. A flash of red caught her eye, a patch of wild raspberries. She plucked one and ate it, letting the sweet and tart flavours mingle on her tongue.

They would love these tonight. Celine wished she had something to carry them in. Rummaging in her pocket, she drew out her kerchief. That would have to do. Spreading it out on a rock, she filled it with the plump, juicy berries then lifted it gingerly by the corners, being careful not to bruise them.

A rustling sound behind her caught her attention. Still nervous after her encounter with the bear, she spun around, eyes scanning the trees for danger. But she was met with silence. Too much silence, she realized. Even the wind had died down, leaving everything abnormally still. Checking behind her, she quickened her pace; a strange prickling sensation at the back of her neck warned her that something was amiss.

A crashing through the trees broke the silence, and Celine ran, dropping the kerchief, letting her berries roll the ground and leaving a splotch of red. Celine scrambled over the sharp rocks. Whatever was behind her was catching up quickly. When she reached a smooth section on the trail; she risked a glance behind her. Fear gripped her heart. It was Karl, face twisted in a snarl as his legs covered the ground at an unnatural speed. Even though Celine was quick, he was gaining on her as if she were standing in place. Still running, she reached for her sword, clasping her hand around the cold metal. She spun around, ready to take the offensive when her arm froze. Karl was pointing his finger at her as he moved, arm outstretched, eyes focused on her as he chanted. Celine struggled with all her might, but he had trapped her arm as if in a vice—she couldn't even twitch a finger.

This is it, Celine thought, eyes frozen open. Just then, Karl tripped over a loose rock, letting his concentration waver. Celine's arm shot forward, propelled by the force she had been putting into it. Using all her skills, she balanced herself, just getting in a clumsy strike on his torso. A shock went up her arm, stinging like a swarm of bees. Her eyes watering from the pain, she struck again, this time aiming for the hand that still pointed at her. Again, came the stinging sensation, this time stronger. But her attack was effective. Through the tears blurring her eyes, she saw him falter, thrown back by the force. Frantically, she threw herself forward, pushing through the pain, but she was too late.

Karl had gathered himself, even as he staggered back. His eyes glittering with anger; he raised his hand again, the force clashing against her sword. A bolt of energy shot through her, agonizing pain making her vision fuzzy around the edges. This was stronger than anything she had fought before. Grasping the sword in both hands, she raised it above her head; then, knowing he would send his power to her sword, she flung her leg up toward his chest. Arms pinwheeling, he fell to the ground, but not before he sent another flash of blue light spinning toward her. Celine ducked and turned, zigzagging her way across the rocky terrain as she sprinted toward the trees.

Energy flagging, she faltered toward the thickest of them, knowing she had mere seconds before Karl recovered. She didn't dare to look back to see if he was closing in on her. Her heart pounded, her breath was rasping in her chest, drowning out the sounds of the forest as she pushed her way through a thick patch of underbrush, a spiking branch drawing a long bloody scratch on her cheek. Up ahead, she saw a narrow ravine. If she could just make it to that, she could creep along the bottom and make her way toward safer ground. She slid to the bottom of the ravine, sharp rocks scraping against her as she crashed and rolled to the bottom. Another bolt of light flashed above her head, and everything went black.

CELINE BLINKED, MILKY strands of fog and pain clouding her vision.

"Oh, you're up." An overly cheerful voice roared through her head like a hammer.

"Where am I?" Celine struggled to sit up, the fog gradually clearing to reveal her surroundings. She put a hand to her aching head. She realized she was lying on a large, padded seat, covered with furs, clutching the soft strands with her free hand.

"You're in my hunting lodge." A figure came into view, tall, with wide shoulders and dark hair.

"I am?" Celine rubbed at her head, wincing at the fierce pain that pounded behind her temple. "How did I get here?"

"I brought you here." The figure came a little closer, and Celine focused on the face that hovered over her. There was something vaguely familiar about it. Her eyes wandered around the room, and she wondered how she arrived in a hunting lodge.

"I found you on our land; you were lying at the bottom of the ravine. Do you have any idea how you got there?" The man's deep voice soothed her with its rhythmic cadence.

Celine strained her memory, trying to clear her thoughts, but they remained elusive.

"Never mind, it's clear you've been through quite a time of it. Here, drink this; it will help you feel better." He handed her a steaming mug, which she took cautiously in both hands. It smelled sweet, like apples and cinnamon. Celine took a tiny sip, letting the tartness clear the fog.

He stood patiently, waiting until she finished the last dregs. She looked around, her head a little clearer. *Whoever this lodge belongs to is clearly part of the nobility*, she thought, taking in the finely crafted furnishings. Paintings hung on the wood-beamed walls, and soft warm rugs covered the floorboards.

"Feeling better?" His smile was genuine and kind.

"Yes, thank you. I'm so sorry to impose on you like this." Celine was suddenly aware of her grubby state.

"Nothing to worry about, I don't have many guests here, but the ones I do are most welcome. You can call me Alex."

"Well, Alex, thank you for your hospitality. I really have to be going though." Celine knew... somehow.... that she had to be somewhere urgently, she just didn't know where. She attempted to stand up, but overwhelmed by dizziness, she fell back to the bench.

Alex reached out to steady her, his hand warm against her shoulder. "You don't have to go just yet. Stay a while until you feel better."

"Thank you." Celine attempted a watery smile. She lay back down on the furs, watching the fire in the great stone hearth. A spark shot out, sending a flash of recognition shooting through her memory. *What had I been running from?* she wondered, focusing on the licking flames.

"Someone was chasing me," she murmured, letting the warmth sink into her bones. Her eyes flicked to his, noticing for the first time the long lashes that fringed them. "Someone dangerous—I needed to warn them." She pressed her hand against her eyes, sorting through her muddled thoughts.

"I didn't see anyone near you." Alex rubbed a finger against the golden circle around his finger. "Had they been chasing you for long?"

Celine closed her eyes again as she concentrated, distracted by an unfamiliar flutter in her stomach that responded to his nearness. "I was fighting someone—I had a sword. Did you find it?" She opened her eyes, searching his face for answers.

"I did." Alex reached under the seat and drew out the sword, its gleaming handle scattering shards of light around the room. He lay the weapon carefully across his knees. "It's a fine piece." He ran a finger down the etchings carved into the blade. "Where did you get a sword like this?" His dark eyes met hers, full of curiosity.

Celine lowered her lashes; swords were usually reserved for the nobility, "My brother taught me how to use a sword," she answered. "I found out I was good at it, and it gave me an escape, something I could do that was mine." How she knew this was a mystery to her. She shifted restlessly, feeling the weight of his gaze.

A door opened behind her, creating a welcome distraction from uncomfortable questions. "She's awake." A woman bustled in, apple shaped cheeks rosy with smiles. "How are you feeling, my dear?" She pressed a warm hand against Celine's cheek. "I hear you've had quite the ordeal; you must be hungry. I'll bring you something from the kitchen." She swooped up the mug, using the cloth from her apron to wipe away the ring of moisture left behind.

"Thanks, Galia." Alex shot the woman a warm, grateful look.

Before she knew what was happening, Celine was being seated at the vast wooden table in the warm kitchen, tucking into a plate filled with sausages, eggs, a delicious fried bread, grilled mushrooms and large slices of ham glazed with golden honey.

"How are you feeling now?" Alex cut into his ham.

Celine swallowed a mouthful of eggs, "A lot better. I just wish I could remember what happened."

"When you've recovered a bit more, I can take you back to where I found you; it might jog your memory," Alex offered, spearing a bit of sausage.

Celine nodded in agreement; the sense of urgency was growing stronger. "Make sure you take Inver with you." Galia, elbow deep in bread dough, turned around, her apron covered in a fine layer of flour dust. "Whatever... or whoever did that is bound to be dangerous." She looked pointedly at the large bruise blooming on the side of Celine's face.

"Inver?" Celine took another bite of the bread. It was delicious, crispy and golden on the outside—not something she had ever eaten in Lovan.

"Inver's my knight. My mother sends him here to keep me out of trouble." Alex shot Celine a wry smile. "And Galia makes sure he does it."

"Yes, Queen Abigail worries about him being here alone, especially since you are new to the crown." Galia turned back to her dough, kneading vigorously.

"Oh, you're *that* Alex." Understanding dawned in Celine's eyes as she took in Alex's appearance. She gripped her fork as a memory rushed back— the castle in Iasia filled with golden candlelight and Alex, stiff and formal taking her hand for that first dance.

Alex twisted his lip. "Don't worry, I'm still not used to it either; that's why I come here every chance I get."

Celine flashed another glance in his direction. Here, he seemed so different, more relaxed, his hair tousled, the sleeves of his tunic rolled up, bare forearms resting on the table.

"Enjoy it while you can." Galia frowned as she began patting and shaping her dough into ovals. "Your mother is determined to plan that wedding as soon as possible."

Celine's gut twisted at the mention of the wedding. She studied Alex's reaction carefully out of the corner of her eye as he visibly flinched. Clearly, he didn't recognize her, *not that he would,* she thought to herself. *I look nothing like I did, and we barely even met each other in the first place.* Although Celine was trying everything she could to get out of the marriage, a pang of discomfort pricked at her heart when she saw his reaction.

"Do you *want* to get married?" she asked, tracing at the woodgrain pattern of the table.

Alex sighed. "I'm not against it; I mean, I did plan to marry... eventually. But it would have been nice to make my own choice. My mother can be a bit... pushy. I mean, Celine's a very nice girl; I've only heard good things about her..."

Celine avoided his gaze. If she were to be completely honest with herself, she had given little thought to Alex's feelings on the matter. But he was right about one thing, Queen Abigail had been the element pushing the two of them together.

"Couldn't you just say no?"

Galia laughed, leaving a streak of flour on her cheek when she wiped her eyes with the corner of her apron. "Not to that woman."

Alex nodded. "It is very difficult to say no to my mother when she has her mind set on something. I tried, of course, but she told me it was for the good of the kingdom. And she was right; it's hard to say no to that." He pushed his plate back and stood up. "Galia will take you to get your cloak, and then we can go."

CELINE STUDIED HER face in the mirror. Galia had taken her to a large cheerful guestroom to change out of her soiled clothing. Large windows lining one wall let in sunlight that streamed across the floor, highlighting the wood until it shone gold. Long green curtains hung from the windows, with cushioned chairs on either side of them.

Aside from the large bruise that covered one side of her head, she was looking more like her old self than ever. The potion Cherry had given her must be wearing off. She crinkled her brow—trying to follow the thread of the thought before it drifted away. She leaned closer, the cropped hair was turning into a halo of golden curls that sprung out in every direction.

"Cherry," she gasped the word aloud, as a host of memories came flooding back. Cherry... the collar... Karl. *Karl. I have to stop him before he gets to the others... If he hasn't already.* She glanced out the window. Hours had passed since she had fallen into the ravine.

"Alex." She rushed from the room, banging the door against the wall in her hurry.

"What's wrong? Are you all right?" Alex's face filled with concern as Celine came barrelling into the room. He held her by the arms to stop her from crashing into him.

"I have to get back. There are people in danger." Eyes wide with distress, she sat on a nearby chair and began shoving her feet into her boots.

"Inver and I will take you." Alex sprang into action. "I'll tell Inver to ready the horses. I'm assuming you can ride?"

"I can." Celine strapped on her sword. "We'll be going toward the lake. There's a group of people camped there. At least, I hope they're still there." Icy tendrils crept down Celine's spine as she wondered what havoc Karl might have caused her friends.

Celine explained the situation to the best of her ability as she followed Alex to the stable where Inver, a tall giant of a man, was saddling the horses. "Are you sure you're up to this?" Alex' voice was uneasy. "Inver and I can go if you give us directions."

"No, I want to make sure they're all right." Celine was already swinging into the saddle.

Following Celine's directions, Inver led them toward the lake, and in less than thirty minutes, they rode into the camp. Tommy recognized Celine first and ran to meet them. "I was so worried about you, miss." His brown hair flopped in his big brown eyes. "What happened to you?" He eyed the bruise on the side of her head.

"Just a fall." Celine glossed over her injury. "Where's Brainard and Gerta? There's something urgent I need to tell them."

"Here." Brainard strode toward her with the ever-present Miranda two steps behind.

"It's Karl. He knows where we are."

"He was here already," Brainard answered. "Luckily, we fought him off before he could do too much damage, but I think he'll be back—probably with reinforcements."

Celine's eyes scanned the campsite, noticing a still smouldering tent, a wet patch, and a discarded bucket showing where to put a fire out.

"What happened?" Alex asked.

Celine gave an assuring nod to Brainard. "You can trust him."

"It was while you were out," Brainard explained as the trio dismounted, letting Tommy lead the horses away. "He waited until we were eating, so we would all be in one place. Then he used his power to overpower us. Once he hit us, there wasn't much we could do to fight back."

"Did you know he could do that?" Celine asked.

"No one did, not even Gerta. Luckily for us, he came alone. Cathal was out getting firewood. When he heard the noise, he snuck up behind him and hit him with one of his sticks."

"Is he still here?" Alex put a protective hand on his sword.

"No, that's when things got really strange. He must have known they outnumbered him and gave up. He disappeared into thin air." Celine knew by Brainard's expression, that this was unheard of, even in mage circles.

Inver rubbed his chin, a disturbed look in his eyes. "The only way to do that is with dark magic."

"What's the difference between dark magic and regular magic?" Celine turned to Inver.

"Dark magic needs blood, preferably from a mage. The stronger their magic, the stronger the dark magic will be."

"So, if you have no magic at all, can you still use dark magic?" Celine was unfamiliar with the intricacies of mage business.

"It is possible, but your magic will be a lot stronger and more refined if the user is a mage as well," Inver replied. He shifted, turning to Alex. "We're going to have to report this back to court. We can't let him run loose around the country."

"How soon do you think he'll come back?" Celine worried for her new companions.

"He won't want to waste any time now that he's given himself away. We should go immediately." Alex looked to Brainard and Inver, who nodded in agreement.

"There are a few out looking for Celine. As soon as they get back, we can go." Brainard turned to Celine apologetically.

When Inver and Alex went back to the lodge to give the news to Galia, Celine lost no time in pulling Brainard aside. "Prince Alex doesn't know who I am yet....could you..."

Brainard smiled. "You don't want him to know yet?"

Celine shook her head, the words Alex said about the forced marriage still ringing in her ears.

"Leave it with me." Brainard gave her arm a squeeze.

Celine sat on Winston's back as the breeze from the lake ruffled her hair. "I can see why you like it here." She turned to Alex. "It's so peaceful."

Despite Celine's protests, Alex and Inver insisted on accompanying the group back to the capital—something Celine had mixed feelings about. Glad as she was for the extra protection, she was unsettled by Alex and his revelations. Besides, he didn't know who she really was,

and she preferred to keep it that way until she could regain her original
form.

Once they reached the main road, the group travelled quickly and
by mid-afternoon, they were entering the town of Avaglade. A few
cheers went up when they rode into the square; Prince Alexander
waved in response, greeting the various merchants and townspeople
who came out to see him. A few children saw the colourful wagons and
came running— clapping in glee, hoping to see a performance.

"Is it always like this?" Celine asked Fiona, impressed by the
enthusiastic response of the townspeople.

"Usually." Fiona waved politely as she sat tall and elegant on her
horse, her red hair a flame around her. "They just want a show. It's not
like any of them would ever invite us home for dinner."

"I don't know." Celine was hopeful. "Maybe things are different in
Iasia. There was never a ban here."

"It would be nice." Fiona sighed wistfully. "It's wearing when
people are suspicious of you all the time. I'd love to find a place where I
could just settle down and be a part of things Travelling is exciting, but
I don't want to do it forever." Her eyes settled on Bran, one of the fire
dancers.

"What do you think?" Brainard drew up beside the girls. "Will we
stay and give them a show? On our own terms?"

Fiona nodded, her flame-coloured hair catching the light of the
sun. "Just let me get changed."

With practiced speed, the group put on their costumes and painted
their faces; Fiona and Alanna slipping into form fitting acrobat
costumes. Celine watched in awe; she had never appreciated the
back-breaking work that went into entertainment. She clapped
enthusiastically at the end of the performance, promising to herself
never to take a performance for granted again.

"I don't have a tent with me, so I'm going to stay in the Oak's
Head." Alex gestured to the inn across the square.

"Me too," Celine admitted. "I'm not really used to tents."

"Aren't you with them?" Alex shot her an expression full of curiosity.

"I've joined....recently." Celine wasn't sure how much she wanted to divulge about herself at this point. She averted her eyes, clapping and smiling as Bran circled the crowd, twirling his fire stick. Feeling Alex's eyes fixed on her, she turned to face him, noticing how the golden flecks in his eyes caught the light.

"What is it?" She felt that flutter twist in her stomach again.

"I'm glad you can enjoy yourself after the ordeal you went through... and I have this feeling I know you from somewhere... You remind me of someone." His eyes fixed on hers.

"I do?" Celine's heart gave a lurch. She lowered her head, brushing a curl out of her eyes.

"Yes." Alex's eyes were thoughtful.

"And you don't know who?" Torn between being flattered that he remembered her, and worried about what would happen when he found out who she really was, Celine struggled to keep the tremor out of her voice.

"I don't know." Alex looked away, his eyes shadowed. "But it wouldn't matter, anyway. I'm engaged." A muscle in his jaw twitched as he turned away.

Celine drew a design in the dust with her toe. She didn't dare think about what might happen if he wasn't engaged. She sighed, realising how ridiculous it was to be jealous of herself.

"Will we go to the inn?" She smiled brightly at Alex. All she needed was a rest and a bit of time to think, she told herself. Everything would come together in time.

Leaving the group behind, they led their horses to the inn. "Alex," the innkeeper, a hulking man, greeted the prince with a familiar tone.

"Oskar," Alex returned the greeting, reaching out to return the man's handclasp.

"And who is your young companion?" The innkeeper attempted to hide his nosiness by giving Alex a boisterous slap on the back.

"Oh, we're not together—not really," Celine rushed to reply, a blush staining her cheeks at the innkeeper's curious look. "I'm with the carnival."

The innkeeper nodded his understanding, but Celine saw unasked questions lingering in his eyes. "Will you be staying in your usual room, your highness?" He politely averted his gaze from Celine's fiery cheeks.

"Yes. That would be great, and Inver will be here as well. He's out back making sure the horses are all right." The innkeeper nodded, taking Alex's satchel and hefting it over his shoulder.

"Then you can have the red room." The innkeeper directed his comment to Celine as he led her up a wooden staircase to a small but clean room on the second floor.

"Is there any chance of having a bath?" Celine set her satchel down on the bed, hoping for an opportunity to get clean; the dip in the lake had been a while ago, and less than adequate.

Soon, Celine found herself stepping into a steaming bath in a dented but clean tub. Rubbing the floral soap into her hair, Celine dipped her head under the water, closing her eyes in bliss as she let the warm water soothe her sore muscles. Drying off on a rough but clean towel, she dressed and collected Tommy from the stable where he was peppering a bewildered Inver with questions.

"Come on, Tommy." She threw Inver an apologetic look as she dragged him away by the hand. "Time for dinner."

Alex waved from across the room, a smile lighting up his face when he spotted the pair. "Over here." He gestured to the empty seats at his table.

Celine slid into the seat. "The food smells delicious." She lifted a slice of bread and slathered it with butter before setting it on Tommy's plate. Tommy, too polite to ask for any, took it eagerly. The innkeeper placed bowls of creamy soup in front of them, and hungry after their journey, they dug in.

"This is an Iasian speciality," Alex explained as he dipped his bread in his bowl. "We make it with cheese and bacon on top."

"This stuff is good." Tommy dipped his bread into the bowl.

"You can have as much as you want, young man." Alex winked at Tommy, who's mouth was too full to answer.

"I have to ask, if you're not with the carnival, how did you even get involved with them?" They had finished their dinner, including a large pudding glazed with sugar and roasted nuts and Tommy had run back to the stable, presumably to annoy Inver with more questions.

"Gerta asked me for help with... something.... I couldn't say no." Celine traced the pattern on the red tablecloth. "I told them I would help bring them to safety, and I wanted to keep my word." Celine hoped this explanation would be enough to satisfy him.

Alex's amber eyes studying hers. "It's unusual for someone in your position to take much to do with travellers like them. Especially in Lovan. Usually, just tossing a coin or two is enough."

"What do you mean, someone like me?" Celine lowered her lashes to avoid the intensity of his gaze.

"Well, it's clear you're from the nobility. Your clothes might be plain, but they're finely made, you carry a valuable sword, and your horse may not be flashy, but I'd wager he's worth more than the whole carnival put together."

Celine gulped. She hadn't realized her position was that obvious.

"Don't worry, it isn't as obvious as you think. Inver is trained to notice these kinds of things. It's part of his job to be observant."

"Something happened at home." Celine wanted to tell Alex everything but wasn't sure this was the right time. "It was too dangerous to be there anymore, and I had to leave. I hope to get back to fix everything soon as I can, but not until I make sure they're safe." Celine's face was full of determination.

When it came to sharing how she freed the performers from Karl, she was more forthcoming in details. An expression of disgust and sorrow flashed through his eyes when she told him how Karl used the threat of the medallion to coerce them into making money for him. And when she explained about the trade in humans, he recoiled in shock.

"If you need any help with the Iasian side of things, let us know." Alex frowned as he leaned back against the wooden chair. "For now, Inver and I will take them to the capital. We can keep them safe until we apprehend Karl. Then, they can go their own way, in Iasia if they wish, or back to Lovan.

"Now we just need to find him and catch him."

CHAPTER NINE

The sun streamed brightly across the village square, highlighting the venders who had come early to set out their wares. Celine stopped at a stall and bought several packets of sweets, sharing them out among the performers. Still munching, she crossed the square to Alex and Inver, who were waiting with the horses, their breath raising puffs of steam in the crisp morning air. A small tortoise-shell cat ran across the street and darted down the alley behind the bakery, presumably in pursuit of a fat mouse.

"Are they ready?" Alex patted his horse on the neck as the animal pawed the cobblestone street, eager to be on its way.

"Nearly." Celine handed a packet of nuts to Alex before mounting Winston, taking care not to let the sword bang against his side as she swung into the saddle.

After some organizing, which included mediating a spat between Fiona and Arlo, the group set off. Fiona made a point of riding on the opposite end of the caravan from Arlo. Celine rolled her eyes and wondered how long this particular cold spell would last—everyone knew Arlo and Fiona couldn't keep their eyes off each other. Celine and Alex took the rear position and Inver rode in front with Gerta and Brainard. Today, Miranda left Brainard's side and rode in the wagon with the acrobat troupe. They embraced her with open arms, scooting over to make room for her on the front bench.

"How much time do you think we have before Karl comes back?" Celine spoke in a low voice as she whispered to Alex, not wanting to alert the performers to her concern.

"It's hard to say." Alex furrowed his brow thoughtfully. "Brainard seems to think he has a friend—perhaps someone from the Lovanian court—who's helping him. If he's not working alone, he'll regroup faster. Also, I'm getting the impression he's desperate to get these back."

"Wait a minute—the person helping him is from the *court*?" Brainard had mentioned the person was influential, but she didn't remember him talking about the court. "Did he say who he thought it was?" Her mind ran through the members of her father's council. He trusted all of them implicitly; Celine had known them all her life and couldn't imagine a single one of them turning on them and their people.

"I don't think he knows. He just—" Alex cut off his words abruptly as he peered at her closely, a deep wrinkle forming between his eyes, "Your eyes look different. I used to think they were a bit greenish, but today they look blue."

Celine turned away, suddenly self-conscious. "It must be the light," she remarked dismissively, brushing her hand through her hair. It was growing faster than ever. Today, it reached nearly to her chin, the weight of it causing the curls to straighten into tousled waves. She gave it a tug, secretly rejoicing in its new length.

Alex seemed to accept her explanation. Riding beside her in companionable silence, Celine took in the surrounding scenery. There were very few trees, instead tall coarse grass and a thick bristling plant covered the steep hillsides. Interspersed with the plants were rocks—giant boulders, grey jagged teeth against the windswept hills.

"That wool is one of our primary exports." Alex nodded toward a herd of sturdy animals scattered across a hillside. A black and white dog lay in the grass nearby, guarding his charges with a watchful eye.

"They're lovely." Celine studied at the animals. "Few people have sheep in Lovan. It's flat where I live, so more suited to cattle. What else do you have in this area?"

"Well, there's the granite." Alex pointed toward a large, speckled boulder near the path. "And the sea is east of here. We use it for trade and there's fishing. Penelope built a massive harbour, and at great expense."

"I remember. Are people recovering now?" Queen Penelope had taxed her people to starvation levels in order to complete her harbour.

Alex straightened with pride. "My mother was a big part of that. She does a lot of projects around weaving and felting; it puts the wool to good use and it gave people a trade to fill the gap. 'Their wealth is our wealth', she always says."

"I like that." Celine smiled back at him, eyes sparkling. She knew her mother would have similar aspirations for the Lovanians.

A commotion on the path up ahead pulled them from their pleasant conversation. "What's going on?" Celine guided Winston to the front of the procession, which had stopped in its tracks.

"What's happening?" Celine jumped down from Winston and raced to Gerta, who was lying on the ground; Brainard and Miranda were hovering over her.

"It's Gerta." Flaming hair whipping in the wind, Fiona moved aside to let Celine lean over Gerta, sprawled out on a patch of grass. Her eyes were closed, and her breathing was shallow.

Miranda propped her head up, applying a strong-smelling compress to her forehead.

"Has this happened before?" Celine turned to Fiona.

"It has, but very rarely. The only time I've actually seen this was when she sees a vision; it was a week before you found us."

That would have been the first time she had met Gerta, when she was Princess Celine. Celine counted the days in her head.

"What did you do to help her that time?"

"There's not much you can do." Miranda brushed back the strands of dark hair curled around her face. "All we can do is wait until she comes out of it." She adjusted the compress. "I'll keep her comfortable until she comes around."

The performers were getting restless, milling aimlessly, and some younger members of the group, including Tommy, looked like they were about to wander off.

"We'll have our lunch here." Celine decided. "And hopefully, Gerta will feel better soon." She cast a worried glance at the sun. Time was soon going to run out, and she didn't want to be stranded in the open.

Fiona brought out bread, sausage, and cheese she had bought at the market that morning and soon they were sitting down to a make-shift lunch. Fiona brought some to Brainard and Miranda, who refused to leave Gerta's side.

"Want some?" Alex handed Celine his flask, "It's just cider," he assured her when she gave it a suspicious look. She took a sip, enjoying the cool liquid that slid down her parched throat. She handed the flask back to him, inhaling the clean spicy soap he used. *Why does he have to smell so good?*

"I think she's waking up," Miranda called to them, distracting Celine from her wayward thoughts.

Gerta stirred, her eyelids fluttering weakly as she struggled to pry them open. She groaned, a ragged, harsh sound, then sat up with a start, a wild look in her eyes.

"Gerta, what is it?" Celine squeezed her hand.

"Dead, so many dead," Gerta mumbled, almost to herself as her legs kicked involuntarily.

"Gerta, we're all here and you're safe. Did you see something?" Celine exchanged an anxious look with Alex, who hovered over her.

A tear ran down Gerta's cheek, and her breathing evened.

"Here, let me make you comfortable." Alex and Celine propped Gerta up on a colourful cushion as Miranda offered her a vile smelling drink.

"I know it doesn't taste very good." Miranda's voice was apologetic, "But if you can get it down, it will help you feel better."

Gerta held the mug in both hands and took a few swallows of the liquid; her face screwed up in distaste at the flavour of the muddy brown drink.

Celine smoothed Gerta's hair back from her face, giving her time to collect herself.

"What I saw was horrible." Gerta's voice trembled, still shaken by her ordeal. "It was all the people he'd taken before. In a group like this, people come and go, and I even though I always knew Karl was up to no good, I didn't know why... or what he was doing exactly. But, he's been selling them—the one's that are strong enough.... and...."

Celine kept rubbing her shoulder, waiting for her to continue.

"He's selling them to other magic users. And they're being drained, their magic siphoned from their bodies. He chooses the ones nobody will miss—orphans, widow, wanderers. But really," here she shuddered, "he's just a middleman. And he uses us as his cover; it gives him a way to travel around and find new people. If someone runs away to join the carnival, no one even thinks twice about it."

"Did you see anything else? Anything that would help us capture him." Celine prodded gently, hoping Gerta would have an inkling of what Karl's future plans might be.

Gerta took a few more sips from the cup, a bit of colour returning to her cheeks. "He was in cold place. There was snow all around him."

"Is he there now?"

Gerta nodded. "I think so. And he was with someone. I heard them talking. He was telling her soon—soon."

"You think he's coming back for the rest of them soon?" Celine asked as she glanced at the other performers.

Gerta nodded, wiping a droplet from her upper lip. "He knows what we're doing... I think they're both coming back, and with all that power at their disposal...." She wiped another tear from her eyes.

Celine turned to Alex, "How long until we arrive at the castle?"

"At this pace?" Alex rubbed his chin. "Two or three days at least."

"That's too long." Celine fingered her sword as she thought. "Do you think your father could send men out to meet us if someone rode ahead?"

"That's a good idea." Alex turned to Inver, who had joined them. "Could you ride ahead?"

"Your highness, it's far too dangerous for you to stay here; you'd be a target as well." A concerned look flashed across Inver's face. "It might be better if you went on ahead."

"No, I'm not leaving them in danger." Alex was firm.

"Well, then, respectfully speaking, your highness, I have to stay here with you. I've sworn to your father to protect you. If I left you and something happened, I would never forgive myself."

"I'll go."

The three swung around as Brainard stepped forward, joined by Cathal. "I'll go with Brainard; I've got a fast horse. If you write the message in your handwriting, we can take it to the castle and lead them back to you."

Minutes later, the performers produced pen and paper, and Alex was scrawling a message to his father. He signed it with a flourish, handing it to Brainard, who tucked it carefully into the front of his tunic.

Subdued, the group moved on. Celine noticed that Fiona and Arlo had made up their differences and were riding next to each other. Arlo tucked a strand of bright hair behind her ear as they murmured to each other. A pang of longing pierced Celine's heart before she looked away, busying herself with her reins. *It would be nice...* she thought wistfully to herself as she sneaked another glance at the couple... *if someone looked at me like that someday.*

"Ready?" Startled when she heard Alex's voice behind her, her cheeks burned.

The pair took up the rear of the procession, this time eyes warily scanning their surroundings for any signs of lurking danger. But all they saw were the sheep grazing on the surrounding hillsides.

"Where would there be snow this time of year?" Celine asked Alex, trying not to notice too much the way the mountain breeze swept his hair back. She sneaked another look, her heart fluttering when she caught his dark eyes looking back.

"In Iasia? Just the western mountains. But their all along the border; it would take ages to travel their if you were going a traditional way. The western mountains are known for their vast deposits of gold and copper, some of Iasia's most profitable exports."

"Do you think that's where he is?"

"It's hard to know, for sure. But what I'm worried that he's found a way to transport himself from one place to another very quickly, using the magic he's stolen. I just wish I knew what he was planning next. Gerta's vision was so patchy." They both looked at Gerta, who clinging bravely to her mule, was at the front of line riding next to Miranda. Heads close, the two were deep in conversation. Gerta beckoned for Celine to join their conversation.

"We were just saying how much Alex likes you; he keeps staring at you when you're not looking. It's a shame he's engaged already," Miranda whispered to Celine.

Celine's cheeks flamed hot. "Yes, that's too bad. I'm going to check how the other's are getting along." She waved and let Winston fall to the back of line, avoiding the way Gerta's knowing eyes were fixed on her retreating figure.

"We'll stop to make camp within the hour." Celine's eyes snapped open. She had been nodding off over Winston's neck. Who, far too well-mannered to take advantage of her lax direction, plodded along, keeping pace with the others. Even from her spot at the back of the procession, Celine could see that the group was lagging, worn out from the gruelling pace they had set.

"There's been no sign of him yet." Celine took another look around at the sparse hillsides surrounding them. The air was cooler here, fresh with the smell of wind and grass. In spite of the bright sun, Celine sensed a shadow. She turned, eyes narrow as she searched for its source.

"Do you feel that?" she asked Alex. A sudden chill seeped into the air and despite the cloudless sky, the air seemed to thicken. Celine shivered, fear coating the back of her throat.

"I don't see anything." Although the words were confident, Alex tightened his grip on the reins and quickened his pace.

A ringing sound filled the air, so faint it was almost imperceptible, accompanied by a metallic tang that filled Celine's nostrils with an acrid sting. Magic.

"Do you think it's him?" Celine looked at Alex, dreading the answer to this question.

Concern clouded Alex's face, "Something's out there. I'm going to find Inver, If we're prepared, maybe we can fight him...he might be strong, but we've got numbers on our side." He urged his horse to the front of the line, speaking in intense tones to Inver, who nodded in response.

A shadow passed over the sun, far too large for a bird.

"Dragon!" shouted Alex. "Everybody run!"

Celine looked around wildly. They were out in the open; there was no cover to be found. The girls huddled in the wagon, and the tired horses, fuelled by adrenalin, took off madly down the rough path, scattering stones in their wake.

There were three of them. Giant grey creatures, with long ugly snouts, covered head to toe in rough scales. Celine had never seen a dragon before. They were mountain creatures and preferred to live as far from humans as possible, rarely venturing far from their territories, which they protected voraciously. She looked on in horror as one swooped low, hovering over one of the horses which screamed in fear as it came inches from scraping long claws along its back.

Leaning low over Winston's back, Celine tried to make herself small as he raced on, squealing when a dragon blew a streak of smoky flame toward them. Luckily, the grass was too damp to catch on fire, and only smouldered, leaving a charred patch of ground behind. Suddenly, Celine felt herself being lifted into the air, the sound of rushing air filling her ears as leathery wings beat against the wind.

"No!" she heard Alex shout as they plunged up into the sky.

The ground beneath her was so far down, the performers were mere specks. Upturned faces stared in shock and wretched horror. Celine closed her eyes against the cold wind that whistled around her. The other two dragons wheeled, following, and left the performers behind. Cracking her eyes open again, Celine saw one of the wagons burst into flames, the blaze filling the air with a billow of smoke.

Celine didn't open her eyes again until she found herself dropped on a patch of rocky ground. Nearby was a cave, the dragon's she assumed. She lay in a heap, preparing to be roasted by another streak of dragon's flame.

"We're not going to eat you, if that's what you're thinking," the voice was rough, gravelly. "Yes, it's me. We do speak human, you know." The dragon lay on the ground, tucking its paws underneath it. "I'm awfully sorry to do this to you. But we didn't have a choice. He took one of our eggs." The beady eyes looked almost apologetic. "I had to scare everyone, of course, but I tried not to do too much damage."

Celine rolled her shoulder's, realizing aside from stiff muscles and windburned cheeks, the dragon hadn't actually harmed her. In fact, he had been quite gentle with her.

"Hugo. Was it really necessary—the fire?" the dragon scolded his companion as the other two landed beside him, tucking their ungainly legs underneath their large bodies.

"Sorry." Hugo lowered his head, folding his wings up. "I got overexcited."

"Well, see that you don't do it again. There were humans inside that wagon. You know we don't like to cause trouble with them."

"Wait? You can talk?" Celine rubbed her eyes in disbelief.

"Of course, we can talk. We are dragons, we speak dragon plus many human languages." Hugo tossed his head proudly.

"Shush, Hugo, this one clearly hasn't been educated about our kind." The other dragon's voice was apologetic.

"Now, we don't have much time. That man will come back soon."

Hugo blew an angry puff of smoke from his nostrils, sending Celine skittering back a few paces. "If he didn't have our egg, Mildred, I'd set him on fire. In fact, I'm still thinking about it." His large golden eyes gleamed.

"Now, now. You know we don't involve ourselves with the humans. Not since... well, you know..." Mildred's voice trailed off as she gave Celine a significant look.

"When did he say he was coming?" the other dragon looked at the sun, now a pink ribbon on the western horizon.

"He'll be here soon. He seemed keen to get this particular human."

"Are you sure we got the right one?" Hugo peered at Celine, squinting his beady eyes into long yellow slits. "They all look the same."

Celine sat up, huffing. "We do not all look the same."

"Of course, you don't, my dear," Mildred's voice was soothing.

"Yes, we did. He wanted the one with the change of appearance potion on them. She was the only possibility—you are a female human, aren't you?" she turned politely to Celine.

"Er—yes." Celine's head was spinning. "But what do you mean, a change of appearance potion? You can see potions?"

"Of course." Mildred wafted a long spiky tail, waving it dangerously close to Celine. "Especially an amateur one like that; I can see it's falling apart on you. Whoever made it was very poorly trained." She sniffed.

"Can you *do* change of appearance potions?" Celine's voice was incredulous.

"Of course, my dear, child's play. All dragons can, but we don't need to make a potion.... we just... do it." Mildred waved a scaly claw.

"So, you can change me back to how I was before?"

"Like this?" Closing his golden eyes, Hugo blew out a stream of blue flame from his nostrils. Celine shied back, falling on the rocks, but instead of the burning pain she was expecting, a cool tingling sensation enveloped her. In an instant, it was over. Celine lifted a hand to her head, feeling the familiar weight that was pulling on her scalp. Her hair had grown back, she realized, the golden strands running through her fingers and cascading down her back.

"Thank you." Eyes glistening with grateful tears, she turned to Hugo. She reached out a tentative hand to pat him on the neck. It was rough like tree bark and strangely hot.

"No problem, it's the least I could do." Hugo gave her hand a pointed look and Celine yanked it back quickly.

A scuffling behind her drew her attention away from the dragons.

"Oh good, you got her," Karl puffed, his cheeks red and winded from his climb up the side of the rocky hill.

"Yes, dragons always keep their promises." Mildred drew herself up, a regal look on her ugly face. "Now where is my egg? We must have it before it gets cold or there will consequences."

"Not so fast." Karl tutted at Mildred, who flicked her tail impatiently. Hand in his pockets, he strolled in a circle around Celine, who put her hand to her sword protectively.

Mildred sat back on her haunches, waiting for Karl to make his next move. "All right, dragons. You didn't have to remove the changing spell, but I'll overlook it. Your egg in is a cave by the lake at the bottom of the mountain. I've left a fire in front of it as a marker. Now, disarm her and you can go."

"Disarming her wasn't part of our bargain." So quickly, Celine thought imagined it, Hugo winked. Then, in a flash of movement, the dragons leapt into the air, beating their leathery wings.

Realizing this was her chance, Celine drew her sword and lunged toward Karl. Turning, he lazily flicked a finger, batting the sword away with a wrench. Gritting her teeth, Celine tried again, this time gripping the sword with both hands and swinging with all her might. Karl smiled, spiteful, taunting. "I have to admit, your tenacity is admirable. You never do stop trying, do you?" he mocked, keeping her at bay with his power.

A bead of sweat rolled down the side of Celine's face as she poised herself to make another blow. He had to have a weakness somewhere, but what could it be? Her eyes ran over him as her mind raced through all the possibilities, and she tried to remember the little—very little—she had learned about fighting with magic.

"Giving up so soon?" Karl took a step closer, confident he had bested her. Celine clenched every muscle, forcing her body to keep still as Karl strolled toward her. One more step was all she needed to put her plan into action.

Holding his hand in front of him, Karl took another step, close enough for Celine to make her move. Stooping down, she picked up a jagged rock, hurling it at him with all her might. Karl snapped up his hand. But as Celine suspected, his magic was only designed for weapons. The rock sailed right through his defences, glancing off his shoulder. "You little hellcat." Karl's face twisted in fury as he raised his hand again, shooting out a shower of sparks.

Celine dodged the sparks, singing the edge of her cloak as she reached down for another rock, aiming for his head, but hitting him in the chest. It wasn't much, but it was enough to distract him from her sword, and she got in a swing, slicing into his leg.

Karl narrowed his eyes, readying himself to fight back, but Celine was too quick for him. She whipped up her sword, pressing the point against his neck. "One move and you're dead." She warned, using the sword to nudge him into a seated position. She leaned in just hard enough to draw a thin trickle of blood. "Now, tell me who you're selling to."

"I don't know what you're talking about." Karl's voice pitched high in desperation as she forced him against the rocky ground. Celine prodded him with the sword. "All right, I'll tell you."

Celine eased the sword enough to let him speak. "Now talk."

"It was Lord Remy."

"Ruben?" Celine was flabbergasted. The tubby little man on Father's council seemed far too innocent for such dark dealings.

"He's obsessed with magic. Once he got a taste for the dark magic, he wanted more. That's what it does," Karl's voice was a whine. A sheen of sweat coated his forehead. "Now let me go," he pleaded.

Celine laughed. "I might let you live, but I'm certainly not going to let you go."

"Well, at least let's leave this godforsaken place. We can go back to the castle—anywhere." Karl worked his throat as he cast a glance at the darkening sky.

"All right, we'll go back to the castle. Now, start walking," Celine urged him up to his feet.

"What, you mean walk? Why don't you just let me get us there with magic?"

Celine needled him with the sword. "I like the fresh air." She said the words dryly, forcing him down the path in front of her. She took off her belt and used it to tie his wrist together. "Now get moving."

Still complaining, Karl began picking his way through the rocky terrain. Just as Celine was scanning the rocks, looking for the easiest way down, a high keening cry tore through the air. Ignoring the sword, Karl dropped to the ground, covering his head with his bound hands.

A shadow crossed the sky; it was the dragons, streaking down like shadows.

"You have cracked our egg." Fury filled the dragon's voice as it swooped low, perching on a boulder.

"No, it wasn't me," Karl insisted, his voice muffled. "It had already cracked when I got it."

"A dragon never cracks its egg," the dragon's voice boomed. "How dare you treat one of our eggs this way, you insignificant little *insect*?" Celine leapt back just in time as a torch of sulfur smelling flame ripped through the air. Karl screamed once; his body jerked violently, and the he was still, his singed form still frozen in its huddled position.

CHAPTER TEN

A ribbon of smoke tinged the air. Celine froze in place, hardly daring to breathe. Spits of fire were still coming out of Mildred's nostrils and Celine came to with a start, beating out the sparks to prevent her cloak from catching fire.

"The egg, is it going to be all right?" she asked, stepping back. In spite of their friendliness, the dragons were more than a bit intimidating.

"It's cracked." Mildred sniffed and a great tear, steaming with sulphur, rolled down her scaly cheek.

"We can't move it if it's cracked," Hugo explained, patting Mildred on the back awkwardly with his giant clawed foot. "We usually carry them in our mouth; it would be too dangerous for the egg."

"I can carry it for you." Fuelled by gratefulness and a desire to help the dragons, the words flew out of Celine's mouth before she could stop them.

"Really?" Mildred raised her head hopefully. "You would do that after what we did to you?"

"Of course." Celine poured as much confidence as possible into her voice. "You did just save me, after all." Celine pointedly ignored the fact that the dragons had mere minutes before professed not to kill humans.

"Hop on then; I'll take you to it." After some effort, Celine scrambled up to sit on Mildred's shoulders, using her cloak as a cushion to protect her from the heat. Dragons were a lot warmer than humans.

"Ready?" Mildred turned her enormous head, batting her huge lashes over her golden eyes. Flapping her wings, she took off. Celine leaned forward and clutched at her neck.

"Sorry. I'm not used to carrying humans." Mildred wheeled in the air, and Celine bit back a yelp as she glanced down. Mildred was soaring at a terrifying height, so high the trees looked like small toys far underneath them. Within minutes, they were at the lake where an anxious Quinn was waiting for them, pacing outside the mouth of the cave.

"It's all right." Mildred leaned down so Celine could slide off. "Celine is going to carry the egg back for us."

Celine stepped over a pile of bat droppings as she peered into the dark interior of the cave. She choked at the musty smell that filled her lungs as her eyes adjusted to the dim light. There, a pale oval leaning up against a rock, was the egg. The size of a watermelon, it pulsed with a glowing light that showed the jagged crack running up the length of the egg.

"Is all right if I lift it?" She glanced back at the dragons who had poked their heads inside to watch.

The dragons nodded; three pairs of unwavering golden eyes fixed on her. She wrapped her hands in her cloak before taking the egg and nesting it securely in her tunic. Cradling her precious cargo, she climbed back onto Mildred's back.

The moon was rising when they arrived at the lair. Nothing more than a rough hole in the side of a craggy cliff, it didn't look like much from the outside. Celine followed the dragons into the hole, clambering over the peaks of the jagged rocks.

The entrance opened into a giant cavern, a high ceiling arched above a wide sandy floor. Streaks of faint moonlight highlighted mounds of gold and other precious objects piled casually along the walls—more treasure than in the entire kingdom of Lovan, no doubt. In the distance was the sound of rushing water, an underground river.

"Where do you want me to put the egg?" she tore her eyes away from the fantastic surroundings as she turned to Mildred.

"Follow me. I'll take you to the nursery." Mildred led her through a tunnel in the back of the cavern. This one contained a nest, also made of gold coins, in the middle of the floor. Celine carefully settled the egg into the nest, being very careful not to jar it. She felt it vibrate under her hands as she set it down.

Mildred sighed in relief. "I can't tell you how worried I was. We are in your debt." She bowed her head graciously.

"Thank you." Celine shifted uneasily under the weight of the golden eyes. "Could you take me to the castle?"

"Of course, my dear." Mildred hovered over the nest, cooing gently to the egg, still pulsing with its glow. "Hugo can take you."

Realizing she was being dismissed, Celine made her way back to the main cave, pausing once or twice to get a closer look at the treasures piled along the sides of the tunnel. *Truly amazing*, she thought, stepping over a pearl the size of a hen's egg that must have rolled out of position.

"Excuse me, Hugo? Mildred said you could take me to the castle?" Celine turned to Hugo, recognizing him by his size and the darker colour of his scales.

Hugo shook himself, stretching and yawning like a large cat. "Of course. Which are we going to?"

"To the Iasian royal castle."

An hour later, Hugo settled in a large meadow near the castle, startling a few cows as his bulk settled in the field. Not wanting to draw the attention of any guards, Celine had asked Hugo to leave her near the castle, not at it. He accepted her thanks with a cheerful wave of his claw, then swooped away. Celine brushed the worst of the dirt off her tunic, hoping she didn't smell too much like sulphur and headed for the gates.

Ten minutes later, the rain began. Not just any rain, a deluge—heavy sheets of rain punctuated by thunder and lightning. Celine was instantly soaked, chilled to the bone. The downpour drenched her, soaking her hair, which hung from her head in heavy ropes now that it had grown back a significant amount. The wind cut through her wet clothes and stung her eyes. Even on the well-marked road to the castle, it was hard to see the edge of the road. Doggedly, Celine kept going, only pausing occasionally to brush rivulets of water from her eyes. A few times, she was startled by the crash of lightning, so close she could smell its white-hot trail of fire.

When she arrived at the gates, it was late. The windows were dark, only a small lamp in front of the gatehouse still burned. Celine knocked on the heavy wooden door, hoping someone—anyone—would hear her over the din of the storm. Just when she was about to turn away, the door cracked open.

"State your business, please." A guard stood at the door, his bleary eyes clouded with sleep.

"I'm here to speak to King Ruben and Queen Abigail," Celine managed to get out through her chattering teeth. "It's Princess Celine of Lovan."

"Princess. What are you doing outside? I'll take you to your room immediately." The guard snapped a salute, instantly recognizing Celine.

Dripping muddy puddles on the polished floor, Celine followed the guard down the labyrinth of passages leading to the guest wing.

"Here you are." The guard opened the heavily carved door.

"Your highness?" the guard turned questioningly toward Celine as a compact form sat up on the bed.

"What's going on?" her doppelganger clutched at the lace neckline of her nightdress, blue eyes wide.

Flustered, the guard flicked his eyes from one girl to the other.

"This is highly unusual," he muttered, out of his depth.

"She's an imposter. I'm Celine." Swiping a strand of sopping hair out of her eyes, Celine nearly cried in frustration. How had she gotten here so soon? Even with the delays, she assumed she would have at least a few days of a head start.

"Sorry, your highness, it looks as if there has been some sort of mix-up," he apologized to the girl in the bed as he took Celine by the elbow, steering her away from the door.

"But, *I'm* Celine," she protested, her heart sinking as he closed the door firmly.

"Shh... you're disturbing the guests." The guard gripped her arm in warning.

"But, I'm the princess, not her." Celine stomped her foot. She thought now that she looked like Celine again, everything would be easy, but apparently, she was wrong. "Wait, where are you taking me?" The guard led her down a series of staircases. The hall was becoming narrower as the paintings and rugs gave way to bare, utilitarian walls.

"We can't have you bothering the princess." The guard manhandled her into a small, windowless room with only a plain desk and two chairs to break the sparseness. "Sit here." He pointed to one of the chairs and lit a candle before leaving, snapping the lock into place behind him.

With only the flickering light for company, Celine slumped back in the chair to wait. Minutes turned into hours as the candle finally sputtered out, leaving Celine in complete darkness.

A scraping of a key in the lock alerted Celine. Someone was coming back. Rubbing the exhaustion from her eyes, she sat up in the chair.

"So, you say you're the princess?" An older man accompanied the guard. Celine recognized his neat grey moustache from her time on the diplomatic visit.

"Hello, General Neville," Celine greeted him as he pulled the chair up to the desk, steepling his fingers underneath his chin.

"I must say, you do favour her." His keen eyes scanned Celine. By now her hair had dried and although tangled, its golden length shone with its former brightness.

"I don't favour her, I *am* her." Celine tried to hold back her frustration, knowing that expressing her anger wouldn't get her any closer to her goal.

General Neville leaned forward, his iron-grey hair painfully tidy even for this early hour. "We'll take you to Ruben and Abigail after breakfast. They'll decide what to do about this—ahem—unusual situation..." He eyed Celine's sword cautiously. "If you could leave your weapon with us, Lydan here can find you a place to sleep for the night."

"Thank you." Celine handed over her sword and followed Lydan toward the guest wing. Dawn had broken the darkness, giving way to a pale, grey light. He took her to a room at the end of the hallway, one with three guards posted outside. *They aren't taking any chances*, Celine thought as she wondered if they had done the same to Cherry's room. Exhausted, she fell into a dreamless sleep, only stirring when she heard a knock at the door.

Celine sat up, shielding her eyes against the sun that streamed through the open curtains. "Hello there." She addressed her comment to the brown-haired girl who was flitting through the room, building up the fire and fluffing cushions.

"Good morning, your highness." The girl turned, a wide smile on her face.

"Louise?" Celine recognized the girl as the one she had run into in the hallway.

The girl curtsied. "I'm awfully glad to see you back."

"You know it's me?" Tears of joy and relief sprang into Celine's eyes.

"Oh, yes." Louise smiled shyly at Celine. "Whoever that other person is might fool the nobles and the king and queen, but she doesn't even try to hide who she really is around us. Silly girl. We knew right away."

"But *how?*"

"Do you remember the night of the ball? When you stopped to help me pick up my tray? It was my first day here, and that meant the world to me. Well, that other girl—whatever her name is—she would never do a thing like that. She's nothing like you were; she's made at least five of the serving maids cry already, a few of them refuse to even go near her anymore. Of course, in public, she's as sweet as anything—please this and thank you that." Louise sniffed before continuing on. "You can't imagine how relieved we were when we heard the news that you had arrived last night. That's why I volunteered to come help you this morning."

"Volunteered?"

"Oh yes, General Neville wasn't going to send anyone; she has him fooled too, but we know if you're going to have a chance against her, you'll need our help. The dressmaker is going to come up later and fit you. It shouldn't be hard; she's been in with the other one all week, You're the same size. I'll get you a bath and send in Ari before you go out; she's the best with hair." With another curtsy, Louise left, closing the door behind her with a click.

A few hours later, Celine was ready. She had been bathed and primped as never before, her hair coiled and pinned into smooth curls and her borrowed dress, one of gold silk, shining and smooth.

"You're beautiful, your highness." Louise's eyes filled with satisfaction as she looked at Celine. "They'll know for sure now that you're the real princess. There's only one more thing." Louise into the drawer of the vanity and pulled out a velvet-covered box. Inside was a delicate headpiece, sparkling with diamonds and sapphires. The deep blue of the stones matched Celine's eyes perfectly. Settling it on Celine's head, she stepped back.

Strengthened by the encouraging words and the weight of the tiara on her head, Celine opened the door.

"I'm ready." She signalled to the guards, then accompanied by all three of them, Celine swept down the hall to them to audience room. She paused in the doorway. A long aisle stretched before her and at the end of it, King Ruben and Queen Abigail sat on their dais, flanked by the two princes. Celine swallowed back her fear and made her way toward them. Heads turned as she passed through the crowd. News of her predicament must have spread because curious citizens packed the audience hall, all wanting to get a look at the mirror image princesses. Out of the corner of her eye, she caught sight of Fiona and Cathal. She must have changed more than she thought; Celine realized with a pang that they didn't recognize her. Straightening her spine, she continued on, dropping into a deep curtsy at the base of the throne.

"Your majesties," she murmured as she rose and took her place in the empty seat beside them.

The gong sounded, and heads turned back to the doorway. Cherry—as Princess Celine—was announced. Dressed in an expensive jewel covered gown, she glided up the aisle, curtsying prettily and taking the remaining empty seat. The crowd whispered among themselves, heads turning from one girl to the other. Even in a country where magic was part of daily life, this was unprecedented. Celine sneaked a look at Cherry, who glared back before quickly recovering—smiling around at the crowd.

"People of Iasia," King Ruben's voice rang out, silencing the murmurs of the crowd. "We have made a decision."

Celine held her breath, waiting to hear what conclusion King Ruben and Queen Abigail had come to.

"Both girls claim to be princess Celine. It would not be fitting for us to make a final decision without input from the royal family of Lovan. As a result, we will keep both girls under protection until we can obtain assistance from Lovan."

At this news, a rumble of discontent spread through the crowd.

"However," King Ruben raised his voice so everyone could hear him above the rumbling crowd, "we will have a series of five tests that the princess must pass. We will pass the results of the test on to the royal family of Lovan for them to take into consideration."

Celine could feel the sweat gather at the base of her spine as she wondered what kind of tests the king and queen might see fit to devise.

"Do you agree?" King Ruben trapped Celine under the weight of his gaze.

"I do." She met his gaze evenly. After all, what else could she say? After Cherry also agreed to undertake the tests, King Ruben turned back to the crowd.

"I will reveal the details of the first test tomorrow at noon. Until then, I will dismiss you." The king waved his hand at the two girls.

Celine stood; it took all her strength to keep her face from revealing her uncertainties. She flicked her eyes to prince Alex, who was staring straight ahead, an impassive expression on his face. The three guards came to escort her back to her room; as she followed them out, she heard the din of the crowd as they reacted to the surprising news.

"How did it go?" Louise was waiting by the door, eager to hear her news.

"I don't know." Celine collapsed on a chair by the window, still bewildered by the strange turn of events. "They're doing some sort of tests."

"Oh, the princess tests." Louise nodded wisely. "We haven't had the tests in over a hundred years. But I can see how they might want to bring them back now. I'm sure you can win. How much can Cherry really know about what it is to be a princess?"

"But isn't that so archaic?" Celine sat at the vanity so Louise could take the pins out of her hair. "What kind of tests are they anyway?" The princess tests weren't a part of Lovanian history, and Celine only had a vague idea about what they might entail.

"There's five tests." Louise began combing out Celine's golden mane, using her fingers to rub out the soreness left by the pins. "Usually, they follow whatever is happening currently—the needs of the kingdom. For example, in times of war, they might have tests of strength and swordsmanship."

"I hope they have swordsmanship." Celine was confident she could best Cherry in a match. "Do you think you can find out what they're planning?" Celine turned to Louise.

"I could try." Louise was hesitant. "But those kinds of plans don't always filter down to us."

A knock at the door interrupted the two girls.

"Sarah?" Celine dashed to greet her lady-in-waiting.

"Oh, I'm so glad you came back." Sarah embraced her old friend. "I thought I was going crazy. You have to stop her; she's completely mad."

Celine's eyes filled with concern. "Are you all right?" she said, noticing the bags under Sarah's eyes and new lines appearing at the corners of her eyes.

Sarah sank down on the bed. "I'm fine, just a bit tired. I'm just so glad you're all right. Frederich and Lucie spoke to me before I left. They hadn't heard from you in a while and had an idea you were coming this way. She talked the council into letting her come early."

"And the people in Lovan, what do they think of her?"

"She has the council wrapped around her finger, and she seems to have fooled your father and your mother. Although she kept to herself at the castle, I think she knew people would find out if she spent too much time with them, so she stayed in her room most of the time. But she wasn't really trying much with the rest of us—you know—the servants."

"Can you monitor her, let me know what she's up to?" Celine searched Sarah's eyes.

"She's secretive, so it's hard to know what she's planning," Sarah admitted. "She warmed up to Lord Remy, though. She even spent a few afternoons in the library with him before we left."

Apprehension gripped Celine. "Did you go to the library with her?"

Sarah shook her head. "She went alone, but he gave her some things—artifacts. That's what I came here to tell you about. She has a locked chest that appeared in the room after she had gone to meet him in the library one day; I haven't been able to find the key for it. You know how I always do the packing and unpacking."

Celine nodded. Sarah had always been responsible for all of Celine's things.

"I think she must keep the key on her person."

"Could you take it while she's in the bath?" Celine tapped her chin thoughtfully.

"No, she doesn't like anyone around when she's bathing. I tried once, to see if I could find it, and she shooed me away. She still thinks she has me fooled, and I didn't want to make her suspicious."

"We'll think of something," Celine spoke confidently but couldn't shake off her concerns about Lord Remy and what strange items he might have had in that trunk. "Let her think you're on her side and keep trying to get into the trunk. And make sure the guards don't see you; I don't know who we can trust yet."

Not wanting to draw suspicion, Sarah slipped out of the room a short time later, taking a tray and keeping her head down as she hurried past the guards.

THE NEXT DAY, THE CROWD in the audience hall had swelled; everyone was eager to hear what the first test was going to be. The crowd was so big, the adjoining room had to be opened up to accommodate, and even then, people spilled out onto the balcony and into hallways. Celine held her head high and wore her most regal expression as she glided up the aisle. Once again, she dropped into a curtsy in front of the king, queen, and the two princes. This time, she was brave enough to look at Alex's face, examining it for any sign of recognition. Her heart sank as he only smiled politely, waiting as she took her seat.

This time, Cherry had arrived first and shot her a triumphant glance as she sat down, a look so fleeting that Celine wondered if she had seen it at all.

King Ruben nodded to the uniformed man standing beside the throne. Unrolling an official-looking parchment, he began to read.

"The princess tests will comprise the following five tests. Test one—strength—sword play."

Celine nearly squealed in delight—everyone knew she loved the sword; there was no way Cherry would ever win that test.

"Test two—knowledge." Celine wasn't sure what kind of knowledge they were looking for. However, she was confident she had been well trained for her position. That one shouldn't be too hard either.

"Test three," the aide continued in an important voice, interrupting Celine's thoughts. "Diplomacy and politics. It will require the candidates to go through a series of situations to display their diplomatic skills and abilities. Test four, grace. It will require the candidates to show their grace in dancing, deportment, and talents. And finally, test five. Heart. The candidates will have to show they have the heart of a princess."

Celine wrinkled her brow. The first four she was fairly confident about, but the last test was a mystery to her. Celine pressed her lips together in determination. She would just have to do her best—she hadn't come this far to lose." Celine slid her eyes to Cherry, whose face was serene. *Like a princess,* Celine thought bitterly to herself, turning her attention back to the audience hall. She scanned the crowd, her eyes resting on a familiar face. Gerta—wrapped in a colourful shawl—

smiled encouragingly at her. But before Celine could signal to her, the girls were being dismissed. Every eye bored into her as Celine somehow made her way back down the aisle, forcing her eyes to focus on the doorway ahead.

THE NEXT MORNING WAS bright; not a cloud marred the clear blue sky as Louise helped Celine dress for the sword competition. A leather tunic fitted to her measurements and soft breeches gave her the flexibility she would need for her manoeuvres.

"Eat this." Louise pushed a plate across the tray—until public interest died down, the girls' meals were being brought to their rooms. Celine's stomach rolled at the sight of the heavy food; she could never eat eggs, sausage, or bacon in this state. Knowing she needed her strength, she took a cup of tea with plenty of milk and sugar and nibbled a piece of toast. It felt dry and powdery in her mouth despite the butter and marmalade Louise had slathered on it for her.

Pulling on her boots, she flipped the simple braid over her shoulder and followed the guards as they led her toward the arena. Cherry was already there, and Celine reeled in shock at the outfit she deemed appropriate for a sword fighting match. Sheer flowing trousers—containing so much fabric they were sure to get tangled around her legs—and a matching top with long floating sleeves. Her confidence boosted by Cherry's apparent lack of knowledge about appropriate fighting apparel, she took the sword one guard handed her.

"Thanks, Hans." She nodded at the guard. Hans's stern expression cracked in a slight smile as he received her thanks.

Celine strode to the middle of the arena, ignoring the crowds of people that pressed up against the railings, all eager to see the spectacle. Cherry was waiting, her hair loose, a golden cloud of silk around her face.

Celine bowed, then got into position, carefully eyeing Cherry for any sign of weakness. A gong sounded, and the match began. Celine raised her sword and sprang forward. To her surprise, Cherry met her, striking back with such speed and precision that Celine reeled back with the force of her blade. A chill ran up Celine's spine; Cherry was good, far better than anyone in her station should be. Celine struck again, aiming for the other girl's left side, hoping they shared the same weaknesses.

A cruel smile crossed Cherry's face as she flicked her wrist. The arena rang with the sound of metal meeting metal. Another clash as Cherry met Celine's sword evenly. Beads of sweat gathered around her hairline and ran down her temple as Celine fought her deadly dance with the other girl. Cherry wasn't even breathing hard. Finally, she tapped the other girl on the left arm. Not a precise hit—but a hit. A fierce expression of fury crossed Cherry's face as she glanced down at her arm. With a shout, she swung her sword violently at Celine. Celine danced back, feeling the breeze from them as the weapon whistled past her head.

Thinking she had the upper hand, Celine lunged forward, but her muscles froze, and she faltered mid swing. Cherry's eyes glinted as lips barely moving. She whispered a few words under her breath. Celine struggled to move her arms but couldn't; it was as if they were stuck in a thick syrupy liquid. A moment later, and her sword was lying on the ground.

"And here is our victor." The weapons master lifted Cherry's arm in the air, showing she was the winner of the match.

Celine's heart sank as she realized no one knew Cherry had cheated. Knowing no one would believe her if she complained, her eyes searched the arena, hoping someone, anyone, would stand up and say something. The crowd was cheering, assuming Cherry was the clear victor of the match.

Celine reached out her hand to give Cherry the victors handclasp. When their hands touched, a strange spark ran through her fingers. Magic. This magic was unpleasant, almost sticky as it crept up Celine's spine. She jerked her hand back and bowed to the cheering crowd. Still stinging from the humiliation, Celine left the stadium as soon as was possible. As she was slinking back into the castle with her guards, Alex approached her.

Raising a finger for the guards to wait, he drew her through a side door into a servant's entrance. "Did she use magic on you?" Alex questioned her, a concerned look in his eyes.

"Why do you think that?" Celine didn't think anyone had noticed the strange moment between the two girls.

"I thought I felt something," Alex admitted. "I can sense magic—if it's powerful enough, but I wasn't sure if it was her or someone in the crowd. It happened right when she disarmed you; I assumed it was a motion ward to slow you down."

"It was her magic," Celine lowered her voice. "She used it to cheat. Did anyone else notice?"

"They didn't." Alex sounded almost disappointed. "But I know that you're the real Celine; I only met you once, but I know you well enough that you'd never cheat in a match. I want to help you, but we're going to have to catch her in the act if we want to prove anything. I need a signal so I can tell you apart from her." An apologetic look flashed across his face. "It's just that you look so much alike."

"Like a hand signal?" Celine raised an eyebrow.

"Exactly, or a question that only you know the answer to."

Celine pursed her lips, thinking. "How about this?" She wiggled the smallest finger on her left hand, a motion so slight it was unlikely to be noticed by anyone not looking for it.

"Perfect." Alex nodded. He smiled down at her, and Celine's heart jumped in her chest. "You remind me of a girl I used to know." He reached out to touch her hair. "But her hair was much shorter than yours. And her eyes weren't as blue."

That was me. Celine longed to shout the words. Instead, she took a step back, letting his hand fall away. Alex let her go, his watchful eyes following her as she rounded the corner with her guards.

CHAPTER ELEVEN

Next was the knowledge test. Celine was grateful to learn this test would be spectator free. For this test, the girls were going to be in two separate rooms and asked a series of questions. Knowing there was no way to prepare for this test, Celine went out for a walk in the garden. Self-conscious about the trio of guards that trailed behind her, she took the path leading toward the informal section of the garden and sat beside the duck pond, watching absently as a family of ducks approached her, hoping for treats. "Sorry, I have nothing for you." Celine told the disappointed birds who, after quacking at her feet for a few minutes, left, waddled back to the water. Celine sat on the grass, plucking a blade and twirling it between her fingers.

"There you are." Gerta approached, another colourful shawl flapping around her shoulders.

Celine felt her guards tense up as Gerta approached. "It's all right, she's a friend," she assured them as Gerta sat next to her.

"I saw that we don't have to worry about Karl anymore." Gerta pushed wild waves of hair away from her face.

"That's right." Celine plucked another blade of grass, admiring how the light shone through the green.

"I've told the rest of the performers who you are." Gerta's kind eyes met hers. "We're all on your side."

"How is everyone?" Celine asked. "Did everyone make it here safely? Is Tommy all right?"

"Every last one of us, thanks to you and Prince Alex. Alex talked to King Ruben, and he's letting us stay in the shipbuilder's cottages until we can get on our feet. And he gave Tommy a job in the stable."

"That's wonderful." Celine momentarily forgot the stress of the upcoming test. She would have to make a point of visiting Tommy later on.

"Yes, some of us have already found work." Gerta's face filled with pride. "Cathal is going to go on one of the trade ships; he said he always wanted a chance to get back to the sea. And Brainard is taking a position in the castle, Miranda as well."

"How about you?" Celine turned to Gerta.

"I'll be all right," Gerta assured her. "I have my gift. It will be easier here without all the opposition. And the cottages are pleasant, much nicer than the tent."

"Have you been able to...to see what's going to happen?" Confidence shattered by her recent defeat, Celine searched Gerta's eyes, hoping for a ray of hope.

Gerta shook her head, a regretful look in her eyes. "No and believe me, I've tried. I only ever see glimpses of things as it is, and your future is cloudy at the minute. If only I could see more clearly; I feel so responsible for what that girl has done to everyone." Gerta clutched her shawl around her shoulder. The family of ducks swam closer, and Gerta reached in her pocket and took out a scone. Breaking it into crumbs, she scattered it over the water. Celine sat silently, watching the ducks scoop and dive at the crumbs.

"I'll keep trying and let you know as soon as I see anything," Gerta reassured her as she brushed the crumbs from her hands and stood up. "Come, I'll walk back to the castle with you."

Leaving the ducks to their feast, Celine followed Gerta back to the castle.

"It's an invitation to have dinner with the royal family." Louise bustled around, laying out a dress. A gauzy concoction of blue, it matched Celine's eyes perfectly and brought out the gold of her hair. "I have a hot bath ready for you." Louise pointed to the tub filled with lavender and rose scented water. Muscles sore from the previous day's ordeal, Celine sank gratefully into the bath, letting it soak away the pains. When her skin pruned, she wrapped herself in a large fluffy towel and sat at the vanity, letting Louise comb her hair and pin it into a sleek knot on top of her head.

"Sarah sent word that Cherry insisted on wearing yellow, even though it's not your colour, so we brought you the blue dress. It's your best colour." Louise ran a critical eye over Celine as she patted a stray hair into place.

"Thank you." Grateful for the care the two girls were giving her, Celine grasped Louise's hand, giving it a squeeze.

"Well, it's as much for me as it is you. I can't stand the thought of her swanning around this place. She would be as bad as Penelope." Louise pulled out a pair of velvet slippers to match the dress.

Celine gathered her wrap and headed for the dining room, hoping it would be one of the more quiet evenings. King Ruben and Queen Abigail had many friends and loved to entertain; the result being that the dining room seemed to have about fifty guests for any given meal.

Slipping into the room, she groaned to herself as she saw that once again, Cherry had arrived first. And Sarah was right, yellow wasn't her colour. Dressed in a puffy dress of bright yellow, Cherry looked a bit like a seasick dandelion.

Celine slid into her place at the table just as the soup course arrived. Lifting her spoon, she took a bit, letting the creamy flavour rest on her tongue a moment before swallowing.

"Are you ready for the next round?" the gentleman on her left gave her a nudge. Celine remembered him from her diplomatic visit. A member of King Ruben's council, he was an elderly man determined to hold back the hands of time by combing a few wispy bits of white hair across his forehead.

"I believe so, Lord Kareth." Celine took a sip from her glass, hoping she had remembered has name correctly.

"Well, best of luck to you, my dear." Lord Kareth brought his spoon to his mouth, slurping as he ate his soup.

Across the table, Celine felt rather than saw a dark pair of eyes fixed on her. Alex was studying her. When she glanced his way, he took a sip from his cup, wiggling his little finger so slightly it was almost imperceptible. Smiling to herself, Celine raised an eyebrow, letting him know she saw his gesture. She turned back to Lord Kareth, who was asking her another question. At least she had someone on her side.

IT WAS TIME FOR THE test. Twelve heads turned as Celine entered the room. Posture straight, Celine kept her eyes forward, ignoring Cherry's smirk as she tried to tamp down the butterflies in her stomach.

King Ruben cleared his throat. "We'll take you—Princess Celine in the blue—first, and you, Princess Celine in the yellow next." He gestured at Celine, letting her know she would be the first to come before the panel.

Celine clenched her hands together, glad to get the ordeal out of the way as soon as possible. She still had no inkling of what questions they intended to ask—or how many.

Cherry sailed out of the room to the waiting area, accompanied by her guards—who she studiously ignored, making it clear she thought she was above them.

King Ruben's aide brought him a thick book. Opening the book, he ran his finger down one of the pages. "Let's begin. We will ask a series of questions, and you can answer them to the best of your ability."

Celine rubbed her sweating palms down her skirt as she waited anxiously for the first question.

"What are the main exports of Lovan?"

"Fruit, grain, and cheese." Celine relaxed, letting her shoulders unknot. Well versed in Lovanian trade and politics, she hoped all the questions would be this straightforward.

"Name the past ten Lovanian kings in succession."

"What year was the treaty of Valaria signed?"

"Name the dukes of the ten territories?"

The questions came fast and thick, and Celine's head was spinning. But, aside from a few dates, which had always given her trouble, Celine was confident in her answers. But then the questions veered away from facts.

"What would you do if the southern kingdoms asked for an alliance—but in order to join, you had to give up your position on slavery?"

Celine chewed her lip thoughtfully. The Southern kingdoms had long been proponents of slavery, but their rich trade was attractive and would be a substantial benefit to the smaller kingdom of Lovan. Making her decision, Celine spoke.

"We would keep our position on slavery. Why benefit only a few at the expense of many?"

Ruben nodded in response, his expression not giving away how he felt about her answer. "What would you do if a trade route was closed from rockfall?"

"Send the army to unblock the route," Celine answered with confidence. "They're there to help the people; such work should not be beneath them."

After several hours of questioning, Celine was wilting. Finally, after they had exhausted every topic, she was done.

"I think we are finished." King Ruben closed the book. "I will announce the scores after dinner tonight."

Legs numb from hours on the hard wooden chair, Celine stood on shaky legs and left the room, sweeping past Cherry who smirked as she hovered in the hallway waiting for her turn.

Celine sat next to the fire, stretching out her legs and letting the tension seep from her body.

"How did it go?" Sarah had slipped away from her duties while Cherry attended her interview.

"All right—I think." After yesterday's events, Celine was hesitant. That knowing look Cherry had flashed as she passed her in the hallway made her nerves jangle.

"Do you know if she was planning anything?"

Sarah shook her head. "She's showed no signs of it, but that doesn't tell us anything. She knows I'm loyal to you."

"I'll just have to wait until they announce the scores to know more." Celine chewed her lip as she gazed at the fire, wondering if this were to be the end of life as she knew it.

That night at dinner, Cherry was vibrant in a bright green dress. The colour was better than the yellow, but just barely. She laughed often and loudly, the sound grating on Celine's nerves as she waited anxiously for King Ruben to announce the scores.

When the pudding was away, King Ruben stood, ringing his glass to get everyone's attention.

Celine hardly dared breathe as she clenched icy hands together, waiting to hear the announcement.

"The winner of the interview round is, he paused for effect. The Celine in the blue dress."

A sense of relief washed over Celine. Finally, luck had turned her way. She leaned back, letting her pulse slow and the heaviness lift from her shoulders. Cherry glowering at the other end of the table, not trying to hide her disgruntled expression. Celine caught Alex's eye, and he smiled encouragingly at her. She felt her pulse flutter in response, glad at least one person in the room knew who she really was. Even though she was not here to marry Alex, in fact quite the opposite—she reminded herself. She was here to break off the engagement; she could hardly develop feelings for him now. She dragged her eyes away from

Alex and turned to converse with her neighbour, the middle-aged wife of a council member who proceeded to inform Celine in great detail about the activities of her five children.

CHAPTER TWELVE

Celine sat by the window watching the rain chase rivulets down the glass pane. Sleep had not come easily the night before, and her eyes were gritty and sore from lack of sleep.

"Here, take this for the cold." Louise draped a fur-lined cloak around Celine. She snuggled into its softness.

"Did you hear anything from Sarah last night?" Celine couldn't wait to hear how Cherry had reacted to losing.

"She said Cherry was in a state; she had a tantrum and threw some plates." Louise fussed with the cloak, adjusting it just so over Celine's shoulders.

"She did? Are you all right?" The thought of Sarah being in danger horrified Celine.

"And when the guards came to see what the commotion was about, she pretended that I was the one who dropped the tray. Of course, they saw the mess and knew what happened. But what can they do?" Louise shrugged.

"Is Sarah all right?" Celine felt terrible for sweet, timid Sarah.

"A bit shaken, not really hurt. One dish glanced off her, but no actual injuries."

Celine pressed her lips together tightly. Abusing staff was never acceptable. She would have a word with Sarah later to make sure she was all right.

"Let me know if anything else happens," she instructed Louise as she took a piece of buttered toast from the breakfast tray and spread it with marmalade.

"I will, your highness." Louise nodded as she poured Celine a cup of her favourite spiced tea.

Today's event was again in the council room. Celine entered, hoping this test would be less arduous than yesterday's ordeal.

"Good morning." She smiled graciously at the council members, curtsying to King Ruben and Queen Abigail. Cherry's pasted-on smile slipped when she saw Celine, but she quickly recovered, simpering at the council members at either side of her.

"For this test, you will go first." King Ruben gestured toward Cherry. Celine left the room with her guards, who took her to a nearby lounge, a large airy room. Fresh flowers were scattered in large vases. *Queen Abigail's work no doubt,* thought Celine as she sniffed at a bowl of roses. She wandered over to the refreshment table and helped herself to a cup of sweet hot chocolate and a pastry before settling to wait.

Before she could take a single bite of the pastry, she was joined by Lord Merek. Helping himself to a large slice of cake, he joined her on a nearby settee.

"Good morning." She would rather have been alone, preparing for her upcoming trial, but people came first. Lord Merek was one of King Ruben's most trusted advisors, and it wouldn't do to offend him. She stirred her hot chocolate, vaguely wondered why he wasn't in the council meeting.

"I see you're in quite the predicament." Lord Marek took a forkful of cake, making sure the thick cream didn't drip on his fine wool breeches.

"It will all be sorted out in time." Celine kept her expression serene as she took a sip of the foamy liquid.

The door opened and a serving maid came in, weighed down by a heavy bucket of coal for the fire. Stumbling, she tripped on the edge of the rug, overturning the bucket and scattering coal over the richly patterned rug.

"Excuse me." Celine nodded to Lord Merek and set her plate on a side table so she could help. Picking up the scoop by the fireplace, she assisted the maid in cleaning up the mess, even taking a cloth from the refreshment table to wipe the sooty smudges from the rug.

"Thank you, your highness." The maid curtsied as she put the lumps of coal on the fire.

"Of course." Celine wiped her hands on the cloth. There were a few smudges on her dress, but it would have to do for now. Hopefully, Louise could get them out later.

She sat back down next to Lord Marek, who was staring at her with a curious expression in his dark eyes. Taking a sip of her now cooling hot chocolate, she smiled politely. "It's a shame about the weather."

"Yes, quite awful really." Lord Marek stared at the rain still falling from the dark grey clouds.

Presently, an aide came to escort Celine back to the council room. There was no sign of Cherry; she must have left already, a fact which Celine was grateful for.

King Ruben drew out his parchment, asking Celine a series of questions not dissimilar to the ones from the day before. Celine answered them as best she could, vaguely wondering why the interviews split into two tests as it was so nearly identical.

".... the remainder of the event will take place at luncheon," King Ruben concluded as he stood to leave. Luncheon was only thirty minutes away; Celine followed the king and queen toward the main dining room to wait. Queen Abigail was especially fond of mingling before meals, a practice that Celine didn't love but learned to gracefully take part in out of a sense of duty. Accepting a drink from the tray that circulated the room, she took a sip of the spicy, fruity concoction and concentrated on charming Queen Abigail's sister, the duchess of Healy visiting the royal family from her estate in the north.

"How are Arthur and Anna?" she asked solicitously. Arthur and Anna were the childless Duchess's two spoiled hounds; they accompanied her everywhere. She reached down to stroke Arthur, trying to ignore the drool that covered her hand when he swiped his tongue across her hand.

Over the next ten minutes, Celine learned everything about Arthur and Anna—from their health to what time they took their first walk every morning. "In fact, I think he may need a walk now." Duchess Healy handed the ornate lead to her waiting attendant, who led him toward the French doors.

A bell rang, telling Celine it was time to be seated. Still, there was no hint of the what the rest of the next test would be. Celine wondered what exactly King Ruben and his council planned to do. She pushed her thoughts to the back of her mind as delicious smells filled to room. The soup course, a delicate broth with tiny floating vegetables cut into fanciful shapes, was served. Celine managed to calm her nerves and keep up her end of the conversation as she nibbled on the warm bread served with the soup.

After the final course, King Ruben and Queen Abigail stood, signalling the end of the meal. Celine still had no idea what the test was going to be. She sneaked a look at Cherry, who was busy batting her eyelashes at Prince Alex and fussing with her voluminous skirt. Prince Alex caught her eye and winked. Celine relaxed internally, and she returned the cheeky gesture with a wink of her own. *How did he know it was me,* she wondered to herself as she wound around a chatting couple, making her way to the door.

Celine learned from her guards, whom she had gradually worn down with friendliness and extra scones from the kitchen, that the results were going to be announced later that evening. Since they had not summoned her to dinner, she would have to wait until morning to find out how she had fared in the latest challenge.

Her feet whispered on the carpet as she entered the room. Waiting for her in the big chair next to the window was Gerta.

"I hope you don't mind that I let her in. She said it was important." Louise turned her lips down in apology.

"Not at all." Celine assured her, rubbing her neck to ease the tension.

"I had a sighting," Gerta spoke bluntly, not bothering with any pleasantries.

Concerned by the serious tone in Gerta's voice, Celine leaned forward to hear what she had to say.

"Cherry has the sceptre. And she plans to use it against everyone. The only way you can stand against her is to find it and use it yourself."

Celine gasped. "How did she get it?" Celine's sister-in-law, Lucie, could wield the Lovanian sceptre, but she had magic. Celine hadn't a drop of magic to her knowledge and hadn't even dared touch the object, although she had seen its power displayed on several occasions.

"Did you see what she is going to do with it?"

Gerta closed her eyes briefly. "I saw—destruction. She's determined to take this crown at any cost. You need to get it away from her if you have any chance at all."

"Even if I win the competition?"

"Yes, especially if you win the competition. Of course, they'll make the final decision on that when the Lovanians arrive. I'm not sure she realizes that yet. But what I do know is that she's smarter and more ruthless than I ever thought she was." Gerta's face was sad, thinking back on all the time she had spent taking care of the other girl.

"Louise? Do you know if you can find out where she keeps it? If you talk to Sarah, we'll break in and get it that way if we have to." Celine pressed her lips together. Enough was enough; her family and the Iasian royal family had poured their lives out for their citizens; she wasn't about to let someone take that away.

"Yes, your Highness. I'll talk to Sarah when Cherry goes for her walk. She usually takes one every evening."

"Thank you for coming, Gerta; I know this is hard—you two were close." Celine leaned forward and touched the woman's hand.

"Of course, my dear." Gerta squeezed her hand. "And wear the blue dress at the ball tomorrow. It's his favourite." She winked as she drew her colourful shawl around her shoulders and stood to leave.

"Ball?" Celine furrowed her brow, but Gerta had slipped away.

"That must be the grace part of the competition." Louise clapped her hands in excitement.

Sure enough, that evening, a formal invitation written on the Queen's distinctive crested stationary slid under the door to Celine's room.

"Not much notice." Celine grumbled as she scanned the thick cream card. Dressing up wasn't her favourite part of royal life.

Louise spent all afternoon preparing for the ball; the seamstress was in to make last-minute adjustments to Celine's dress—a splendid gown of midnight blue silk.

"It's really lovely." Celine was used to having magnificent gowns, but this one was truly special. She ran a hand down the soft silk, admiring how it shone under the light.

"This colour suits you." The seamstress spoke through the pins in her mouth as she tucked the fabric around Celine's frame. "Prince Alex won't be able to take his eyes off you."

Celine's heart gave a thump at the thought of Alex seeing her in this beautiful dress. *You don't want to marry him*, she reminded herself sternly, struggling to remember why she had been so opposed to him in the first place. If only Queen Abigail had allowed them to get to know each other a little better in the first place, all of this could have been avoided.

The next morning, Celine woke early to go to the practice arena.

"Don't get any bruises." Louise called after her anxiously as she strode down the hallway, followed by her guards.

It felt good to move. Celine hadn't practiced since Cherry had bested her in the test, and her muscles rejoiced as they flowed through the movements of the routine. Lifting her borrowed sword, she spun across the floor in a blur of motion.

"Mind if I join you?" she nearly dropped her sword.

"Of course not." Celine grinned at Alex, who wielded his own sword, a shining weapon with gold inlay on the handle.

"Are you sure this is such a good idea?" A guard stepped forward, disapproval written across his face.

"We'll be fine." Alex waved him off.

Taking their places in the middle of the floor, they both got into position. Celine's guards eyed her warily, preparing to intervene.

Despite Celine's smaller size, they were evenly matched. Alex got the first point when he distracted her with a feint—one of the oldest tricks in the book. However, she soon rallied and struck back, sending him back several paces.

After a few more minutes of sparring, she won the first match when she flicked the sword out of his hand.

"How did you do that?" he laughed as he picked up the weapon. Side by side, they walked to the edge of the arena, much to the relief of Celine's guards who had looked ready to faint when she had disarmed him.

"Practice. Lots and lots of practice." Celine laughed, her cheeks flushed with exercise and adrenaline. "I've always loved it, and my father knew if I kept up with it, I could defend myself. Frederich taught me everything he knew, and it made me feel close to him when he disappeared. Like he was still there with me."

Alex listened intently as she spoke about her brother. "Were you two close?"

Celine nodded. "Yes, we understood each other like no one else could. What about you and your brother?"

"We are... but our situation was different; we were only a dukedom. Not so much responsibility." Alex wiped his face with a cloth and took a drink of water.

"Was it hard to get used to? All this, I mean." Celine waved her hand in the general direction of the castle.

"Very. No one ever expected Penelope to disappear the way she did. I think I'm still getting used to it in a lot of ways. I guess that's why I try to spend so much time at the lodge."

Celine leaned against the railing. "Your mother and father seem to be adjusting well, though. Your mother fits right into court like she was born for it."

"I think I was the one who took it the hardest. My mother's always liked to organize people, so she's in her element here. But I expected to live a quiet existence—not rule an entire kingdom." Alex paused and cleared his throat, an awkward expression on his face. "I always wanted to tell you.... I'm sorry about what my mother did to you... she didn't give me any warning that she was going to push us together. I could have reacted a lot better than I did." His eyes met Celine with a genuine look of apology.

"It's all right. I could have as well." Celine's heart warmed as her blue eyes met his brown ones.

"I guess, I wasn't expecting it and I didn't have control over anything anymore. I was pushed into ruling a kingdom, and now a marriage. I know my mother means well, but she can be highhanded."

"I'll say." Celine rolled her eyes in agreement.

"So, can we start over? I won't hold you to any agreements you made with my mother; I'll handle her." Alex held out his hand.

"Starting over sounds good." Celine held out her hand to take his, wondering why, since she had gotten the freedom she came for, she felt a pang of regret. His hand was warm and dry; Celine suddenly realized she was holding it much longer than necessary and dropped it like a hot poker. He smiled, then whistling, he put away his practice sword to leave.

"Wait, a minute," Celine called after him. He paused, brushing a strand of dark hair away from his eyes as he waited to hear what she had to say.

"How did you know it was me in here and not Cherry?"

"Easy," Alex replied, voice light. "Everyone knows you're the fastest sword around."

Thoughtfully, Celine put away her own weapon and went back to her room.

"HOLD STILL; I'M NEARLY done." Louise jabbed another jewelled pin into Celine's hair. Tonight, she had arranged it into a fall of golden curls that spilled down her back from a braided crown. Celine smoothed her hands down her dress. Usually, she didn't mind getting ready, but the anxious butterflies in her stomach made it hard to sit still. Louise hadn't managed to learn anything about the sceptre. Sarah had been kept very busy indeed by her demanding mistress.

They also weren't yet informed who the winner of the diplomacy award was, and the suspense only increased her jangling nerves.

"You're ready." Louise stood back and surveyed her handiwork with a proud expression on her face. Celine had to admit, Louise had done beautiful work. Everything was perfect. She slid her feet into a pair of velvet slippers and settled the matching wrap around her shoulders.

"One more thing." Louise took a small bottle of perfume from the vanity. "Gerta sent this for you. She says it's special and you have to wear it tonight." She removed the crystal stopper and dabbed the scent onto Celine's neck and wrists. The heady scent of Jasmine and bergamot swirled in the air. "No one will resist you now."

A few minutes later, Celine stood at the top of the stairs that led to the main ballroom. Her mother taught her to always stand in the doorway until people noticed her before entering a room. "It's important in your station to give your time to people." Her mother had reminded her when she complained about being constantly stared at.

Heads turned as she rested her hand on the rail and glided down the steps, flicking her dress well out of the way to avoid tripping. At the bottom step, a pair of brown eyes met her blue ones. Alex froze as his eyes met hers, an almost tangible spark flying between them. He held out his hand, and she took it, his warm skin renewing her confidence.

Courtiers crowded the room; everyone was there to get a look at the rival princesses, no invitation was turned down. Leading her to a space on the dance floor, Alex spun Celine gracefully into the traditional Iasian ballroom dance. Grateful to her mother for making her learn all the steps, Celine joined the movements, following his lead as her soft blue skirts swirled around her.

"You look beautiful tonight," Alex's voice was a whisper as he raised his arm so she could spin under it.

"Thank you." Celine smiled. "But I know you have to say that to everyone."

Alex grinned back. "I do, but I've never meant it more than I do now."

Celine lowered her lashes as her heart skipped a beat. All too soon, the dance was over, and as was custom, Alex moved onto another partner. Celine had no lack of suitors. People wanted to get a closer look at the phenomenon of the identical princesses. Celine graciously danced with every partner who asked, although she would have preferred to be back by Alex's side, protected against the curious stares of the Iasian courtiers.

Across the room, she spotted Cherry, dressed in a bright green gown covered in a strange salmon lace. Celine wondered why the seamstress had not advised her against that particular combination. It did her golden hair and skin no favours, painting them with a sickly pallor. Cherry caught her eye and glared.

With a start, Celine realized this was it—this was her chance to find the sceptre before Cherry could use it. Why didn't she even think of this yet? She scolded herself for the oversight. But she wouldn't be able to go herself, not under the watchful eyes of her guards. She glanced up to check on them, placed at various points around the edge of the room. They stood ramrod straight; their eyes never leaving her. But.... an idea came to her, and she casually moved toward the refreshment table, dismissing her current dance partner as she informed him she was in dire need of a cool drink.

Several of the castle servants manned the refreshment table and Celine scanned them carefully, looking for one she recognized. That would be her best hope of getting the message to Louise.

There—a slender girl with dark brown hair and eyes serving the punch. She smiled hesitantly at Celine. Pretending to hover over a tray of pastries, Celine caught the girl's eye. "Can you get away for a moment and ask Louise to come—it's an emergency. Tell her to meet me at the staircase," Celine spoke in a low voice to the girl. Responding to Celine's friendly tone, the girl curtsied.

"Right away, your highness." She slipped away, and Celine wove her way to the staircase, hoping she didn't look too obvious to the guards. She waited until the dance started again, then just as a couple moved in front of her, she slipped through the door leading to the hallway. Louise was waiting for her.

"Louise, Cherry's in here and she's occupied. Can you find Sarah and go look for the sceptre?" She lowered her voice so the guards that now hovered in the doorway couldn't hear her.

Louise hurried off and Celine turned back to the ballroom, hoping her absence would go unnoticed by the other party-goers. As she turned, she bumped into Prince Alex, who was standing in the doorway. "There you are." A smile lit up his face. "I've been looking for you. I've done my duty dances, so I was wondering if you would do me the honour." He held out his hand.

The butterflies in Celine's heart fluttered at the knowledge that he had sought her out. "How did you know it was me this time? We didn't use the signal."

"You might have the same features, but everything else about you is completely different." Prince Alex dipped her toward the floor, one hand securely behind her back. "You're kind and the fact that you truly care about your people shows."

Celine warmed at the compliment, knowing it was not earned lightly. She put one hand around his shoulders, leaning in more than was strictly necessary as they swayed across the floor.

"I think I'm not the only one who's noticed." Alex nodded toward King Ruben and Queen Abigail, who were looking their way. "Mother and father noticed the difference as well. One more test and there will be no doubt about it."

"What are we doing for the last test?" Celine was nervous about what trial she would have to face next.

"I don't know. My mother is organizing this one, and she's being even more devious than usual about it," Alex admitted.

Celine worried her lip, wondering if Cherry had any tricks up her sleeve for the next trial.

"Do you know when they're going to announce the results of the last test?"

Alex shook his head. "I was in the council meeting while they were discussing it and they've decided to wait until the end and make a big announcement. His eyes softened as her took in Celine's worried expression. "Don't worry, he stroked the back of her neck with his warm fingers. The truth will come out in the end."

Celine smiled, hiding her fears under forced cheer. "I'll look forward to when it's all over then." She curtsied as another partner— an

Earl— cut in, taking her hand. Alex reluctantly let her hand slide away, his eyes never leaving her.

At long last, the ball came to an end, and the results of the trial were still not announced. Exhausted, Celine climbed into bed and blew out the last candle. Louise had not made an appearance that evening, which was unusual for her. She was nearly always there when Celine was, even sleeping in the cot in the dressing room in case she was needed during the night.

Tired as she was, sleep did not come easy that night; the bed was strangely lumpy. Although Celine was exhausted from the late hour and tensions of the trials, she tossed and turned. Eventually, when grey smudges of light peeked around the edge of the curtains, Celine decided to forgo sleep. She put a warm blanket around her shoulders and went and sat by the window. Louise was still missing, and Celine had to start the fire herself, fanning the embers until it blazed up, warming the room with heat. She rubbed her lower back. Whatever was in her bed to make it so uncomfortable had left her sore and bruised. She wondered if she should let the housekeeper know. After all, other guests stayed there as well and it wouldn't do to have them uncomfortable. After the room warmed, she dressed herself, lacing her gown up as best she could and opened the door, startling the guard.

"Harry, have you seen Louise anywhere?" Celine asked the guard, who was still blinking in surprise to see her awake at such an early hour.

"No, your highness." A concerned expression crossed his face. He knew Louise was too loyal to leave Celine's side for long.

"Could you send someone to go look for her? She never came in last night, and I want to make sure she's all right."

"I'll go; I'm due to shift change soon," Harry offered.

Celine nodded and went back into her room to wait. The sun was soon high in the sky and still Louise hadn't come. Celine went to look for her herself. Limping from the pain in her back, she headed toward the kitchens, guards trailing closely behind her.

The kitchens were busy—it was the breakfast hour and trays were being prepared for all the rooms as well as for the service in the breakfast room. The smell of bacon and toast drifting through the air made Celine's stomach growl, but she tamped down the hunger, her concern for the missing girl forefront in her mind. Not wanting to interrupt their work, Celine waited until she saw one of the maids bringing a tray back from one of the staterooms.

"Have you seen Louise anywhere?" she asked the girl, so startled at being approached by the princess, she nearly dropped her tray.

"No, wasn't she with you last night?" a wrinkle formed between the girl's eyes.

"No." Celine shook her head. "I spoke to her at the ball, but I haven't seen her since."

Celine wished she had never sent Louise poking around Cherry's room. Who knows what sorts of things Cherry might have stored in that chest of hers.

After asking a few more people and not receiving any answers, the knot in Celine's stomach began to grow thick and hard with worry. Celine decided to enlist the help of the guards, who were more than willing to help in the search for the missing girl.

It was over an hour later before Celine arrived back to her room. A now familiar piece of stationery waited for her under the door.

"Audience at 10 am?" Celine read the card. She quickly pinned up her hair with clumsy fingers, realizing she had little time and no one to help her get ready. There wasn't much she could do about the dark circles that hung under her eyes, so she pinched a bit of colour into her cheeks and dashed cold water on her eyes to remove the redness.

"This way; we're going to the king's private chambers for this audience." The king's steward met her at the door.

Celine widened her blue eyes in surprise. Even on her diplomacy visit, King Ruben and Queen Abigail hadn't invited her to the private apartments—their court sanctuary. She followed the steward down the hall toward the private wing. Cherry had already arrived and was sitting stiffly in a high-backed chair. Celine took a seat, looking around with curious eyes. Although stately, it was clear this was a personal space with family paintings on the walls and sentimental knickknacks scattered about. The queen's little companion dog lay on a cushion near the fire, its paws twitching in its sleep.

Queen Abigail sent for refreshments, and hungry from her missed breakfast, Celine was glad to see the sweet rolls, sticky with honey, were still warm from the oven. She took a cup of tea and added milk and a few generous lumps of sugar.

"How did you sleep?" an intent look flashed across the queen's face before she quickly covered it with a polite smile.

"Wonderful." Cherry gushed, leaning forward with enthusiasm. "I think that your bed is more comfortable than my own." She giggled, an annoying sound that grated on Celine's tired nerves.

"And you?" the queen turned to Celine, waiting for an answer.

"I'm afraid I had too much on my mind to sleep very well, Your Majesty." Celine disliked lying, but she also didn't feel it would be diplomatic to complain about the lumpy mattress. Either way, she wouldn't be in it very much longer.

"Oh, dear." The queen's face took on a look of concern. "I hope there wasn't anything wrong with the bed."

"I'm afraid that something might have gotten caught under the mattress. No matter, I can have Louise look under it when I return." Celine took a sip of her tea, hoping she hadn't crossed the boundaries of politeness. This was not a good time to offend.

"Of course." The queen's eyes gleamed.

King Ruben cleared his throat. "Well, I'm sure you girls are wondering why we brought you here instead of to the council chambers." he began. "The truth of the matter is that the final and most important test took place last night."

"You mean there's only four tests?" Cherry's eyes filled with confusion.

"No, the ball was the test of grace, but there was another test after that one."

Celine squeezed her hands together in her lap, waiting to hear what King Ruben had to say.

"It was this." He raised his hand. Between his thumb and his forefinger was a small green ball, about the size of a marble. "I know it looks like a pea. But this is magic. It has been warded with the ability to feel out the true nature of a person's heart."

Queen Abigail took over. "While you were at the ball, one of these was put in each of your beds. The girl who could feel it is the true princess. Celine, that lump in your mattress—was this. You are the true princess." She turned to Celine with a gentle smile on her lips.

Cherry's mouth gaped in shock as an ugly expression marred her features. She stood up, huffing in protest. The king's guards, who had been standing at the edge of the room, were too quick for her. Before she could move, they secured her by the arms.

"Be careful," Celine warned. "She can change form—and she's good at it."

"Don't worry," the king assured her. "They're using copper. It will dull her magic so she won't be able to use her abilities."

Cherry twisted and struggled, shrieking in protest. But the guards soon had two copper bracelets clamped around her wrists. "Take her to the most secure cell," King Ruben ordered. "She's dangerous and trickier than you might think."

"We have a room lined with a layer of copper. We use it for mages, and I had it strengthened after what happened with Penelope," King Ruben explained to Celine. "She won't be able to do anything once she's in there."

"I'm so sorry about everything you had to go through." Queen Abigail's eyes filled with sympathy. "But we couldn't take the chance of getting the wrong person. We designed the first trial to give you the advantage right away. Everyone knows your skills with the sword. She had us fooled until one of our mages warned us about the magic she used in the first trial. We had to go through with the rest of the trials. After that, she showed her hand. We were sure it was you all along; we just needed ultimate confirmation. I'm so sorry you had to go through that ordeal. I'm sure it was terrible." She put a warm hand on Celine's shoulder.

Tears of relief stung Celine's eyes; her ordeal was over. Cherry was gone. Her shoulders relaxed and for the first time since Cherry had taken over her life, she realized she could be herself again.

"Also...." Queen Abigail broke in. "We have decided—King Ruben and I." her eyes flicked to King Ruben who nodded in support. "That we will not hold you to the engagement. It wasn't fair or right to push you into it. I was overexcited, you were so lovely and perfect, and the alliance would have been wonderful. But it wasn't the right thing to do." She held out her hand in apology.

A shiver of disappointment ran through Celine. She had become fond—more than fond if was honest with herself—of Alex over the past week and the thought of never seeing him again sent a pang of sadness shooting through her. "Thank you." She managed a smile as she forced the words out.

"And, of course, you are free to go back to Lovan whenever you wish. I will send a contingent of guards to go with you." King Ruben's face was solemn. "We only wish for good relations between the two kingdoms. Of course, if King Erich is open to the idea, we would still welcome a strategic alliance. But we will go through other, more appropriate channels."

"I appreciate your offer." Celine couldn't help feeling that she was being dismissed. A door behind Queen Abigail opened. Alex came in, seating himself on a settee next to his father. His eyes slid to Celine's, a smile lighting up his handsome features. "Didn't I tell you all along, Father?"

"Yes, yes, you did. I should have listened." King Ruben's eyes twinkled at his son's teasing voice.

A commotion rumbled outside the door, jerking them from the conversation. Alex ran to the door, eyes alert. A guard met him, rushing in and locking the door behind him, panting heavily from exertion.

"What's happening?" Queen Abigail's brow furrowed in concern.

"It's the false princess, Your Majesty. She's turned into an ogre and attacked the guards as they were putting her into the cell."

"But, how did she do it? The cuffs should have prevented that." King Ruben quickly closed the open windows, locking them securely.

"She somehow accessed her magic just long enough to get her wrists to slide through them. She must have known it was her only chance. Once she was in that cell, she could never have used it."

"Do you know which way she went?" Alex paced up and down the room.

"I think toward the guest wing."

"The sceptre." Celine gasped. Everyone turned their attention to her, waiting for an explanation.

"I think she sneaked the sceptre out of Lovan and brought it here with her. She must plan to use it. I sent Louise to look for it last night and she never came back—that's what I wanted to talk to you about..." Celine blinked the moisture out of her eyes.

King Ruben and Queen Abigail exchanged concerned looks.

"Is there a way to get into her room unnoticed?" Celine asked. "The girls thought she was keeping it in a locked trunk. If there's a tunnel, maybe we could sneak into her room."

King Ruben shook his head. "Unfortunately, when Penelope left, she took those secrets with her. We've found a few of the tunnels, but nothing that leads in that direction."

"What is it do you think she wants?" Queen Abigail turned to Celine. "Do you have any idea? Maybe if we made her an offer..."

"She wants everything... the prince, the crown, and the kingdom." The noise in the hall grew louder, shouts of men growing closer. They were almost at the door now. There was a clash of swords, then sudden silence, eerie after all the chaos.

"Where did she go?" a guard shouted.

A scurrying and scratching at the door caught her ear. A small field mouse, with a brown coat and bright eyes, ran under the door. Queen Abigail forgot her dignity and lifted her feet from the floor with a squeal of dismay.

The mouse ran to the middle of the floor and blinked up at them where it began to grow, stretching and oozing into the shape of a woman. But this was not the now familiar form of Celine, or of the girl she had known as Cherry. This woman was much older. She stood tall, magnificent black hair waving around a beautiful face with cold blue eyes. One hand gripped a jewelled sceptre, the unmistakable Lovanian crest carved into its side.

"You." The woman pointed at Celine, eyes blazing with anger. "You ruined everything. Do you realize how long it took us to plan this?" She raised the sceptre. The end of it sparked and hissed, lighting up the room with a fierce glow.

Celine sat frozen in her seat. Her fingers itched for a sword as her eyes slid around the room, hoping to spot something she could use as a weapon. Then she saw it, hung over the fireplace, an old-fashioned long sword, an antique. It would have to do. She averted her eyes so the woman wouldn't know what she was planning.

"Us?" she said, attempting to distract the woman long enough to grab the weapon.

"Yes, us." The woman sneered, an ugly expression marring her beautiful features. "It's been too long since magic has reined free in Lovan, and now that it is, the people are ruining it with their judgmental attitudes. We've been planning this for years. We knew when the sceptre re-appeared that we had our chance." She waved the object, sending sparks shooting across the room. Queen Abigail's little dog whimpered, cowering under the settee.

"But, what did you want?" Celine eyed the woman carefully. If she just took one step to the left, she could dash past her. "We changed the law and lifted the ban on magic. We can't change people's minds that quickly. What else did you want us to do?"

The woman paused, a surprised expression flitting across her face as she lowered the sceptre an inch. "Well, you could make it a crime for people to hurt us, for a start."

"But we tried to do that. I don't know what more we can do to convince people, these things take time," Celine protested.

Cherry lowered her eyebrows as she raised the sceptre again, poising it to strike. Celine gulped, realizing she had lost ground. "What do you suggest we do?" she quickly tried to recover and regain the rapport.

The woman pouted like a small child. "Do you know what it's like for people to hate you, fear you, wherever you go? For them to take their children inside and shut their doors in your face? No, of course you don't. You're the favourite child of the king. Everyone adores you everywhere you go. Even when I looked just like you, you were still the favourite." Bitterness filled her eyes as she glared at Celine.

"All I wanted was to be like everyone else. But if I can't have that, I'll just have to do this instead." She raised the sceptre over her head, sending showers of multicoloured light scattering across the room. A strange tingling sensation swept across Celine. With a jolt of alarm, she realised she couldn't move. Even her eyelids froze in place and her very blood seemed to slow down in her veins. Across the room, Alex and the king and queen were likewise locked in position, a look of horror carved into Queen Abigail's face.

Cherry closed her eyes, muttering terrible sounding words in a strange ancient tongue. Power poured out of the sceptre, flooding the room with magic. She realized this was the end and her heart filled with regret as she thought of the family she would never see again— her parents, her brother, Lucie, and Alex. Across the room, his tall figure was a block of ice. Celine wondered wretchedly what would have happened had they gotten acquainted without the meddling of Queen Abigail and Cherry. It was with a stab of regret that she realised she would never know.

Suddenly, the power stopped, cut off at the source. The thick syrupy air was still tinged with magic, but even that was changing as a light, fresh breeze raced through the room, ruffling Celine's hair and the corner of her dress. Celine heard footsteps, someone was behind her, but she couldn't move enough to turn around.

"Not so fast," said a feminine voice behind her. The rays of light that flashed from the sceptre faded to a dull shine. The owner of the voice stepped into her line of sight. It was Lucie, hand outstretched and eyes focused in concentration on the sceptre.

Cherry's face paled as she realized her weapon no longer obeyed her and her hand shook. The sceptre slid out of her hand and floated across the room to rest in Lucie's waiting hand.

"Enough," Lucie commanded, her voice quiet but firm. The magic disappeared, visibly returning back into the sceptre.

Celine's limbs filled with pins and needles, her body responding to the magic wearing off. A snarl of anger came out of Cherry's mouth when she realized her most powerful weapon was no longer at her disposal. Leaping forward, she wrapped her hands around Lucie's neck. Celine acted quickly. In two steps, she reached the fireplace and grabbed the sword. Spinning around, she held the point to the back of Cherry's neck, just enough to prick the surface of the skin.

Cherry released Lucie a fell back. Alex and King Ruben sprang into action, twisting her hands behind her back.

"We need copper," Alex shouted to the guards who had come rushing in.

"Here," said Lucie, "this will work." She spoke a few words gently to the sceptre and a faint rush of air, streaked with purple, whisked past Celine and twisted round Cherry, binding her hands together.

One of King Ruben's guards brought the bracelet and tightened it around Cherry's wrists; this time making sure there was not even a sliver of space remaining between the metal and her skin.

"I'll go with the guards to make sure she doesn't escape; then we'll talk." Taking the sceptre with her, Lucie accompanied the guards as they took Cherry back to the cell.

Celine sank back into her seat as the door closed behind them. Her head was still spinning from the close call. "Are you all right?" Alex sat next to her; she basked in his comforting warmth and the clean smell of sandalwood that accompanied him. His brown eyes scanned her for injuries.

"I'm all right." Celine took a shaky breath. She realized she was still holding the heavy ceremonial sword and set it carefully down at her feet, wiping her hands on her dress.

"Your Majesty, may I announce the Crown Prince Frederich and Princess Lucie." The steward appeared at the door, bowing deep as he ushered Frederich and Lucie into the room.

"Frederich? How did you get here so soon?" Squealing with delight, Celine embraced her brother enthusiastically.

"We left not long after you did. Father and mother didn't argue too much. I think they were worried something was up; Cherry was acting so strangely. Not like you at all—so when we left, we travelled as quickly as possible. We were so worried about what kind of mischief she might be up to. And it looks like we left just in time." He finished his sentence grimly. "We suspected she had the sceptre with her when Lucie couldn't find in her office."

"Lord Remy gave it to her. He's not as much of an ally as we thought he was." Celine quickly filled Lucie and Frederich in on Lord Remy's unsavoury activities.

"I wondered why he disappeared when Cherry left. He told everyone he was going back to his estate. I was going to ask him if he'd seen the sceptre anywhere."

"Is that where you think he is now? His estate?" Celine asked. "We have to track him down before he retaliates."

Alex shot a worried look toward Celine. "Couldn't you leave that to your father's men? You've done enough." His brow furrowed in concern.

Frederich laughed. "Celine? Leave the action to someone else? Not a chance" He threw his sister a wink.

"Be careful," King Ruben spoke. "Lord Remy is obviously extremely dangerous. Who knows what kind of power he has amassed. When we find him, it's important to strike fast so he doesn't have any warning."

The younger members of the group pondered this advice. Celine, Lucie and Frederich mourned the loss of the man they had known of as a friend and one of King Erich's closest allies.

"Does he have any idea that we know its him?" Lucie asked.

"I doubt it. I just hope that he's gotten away with it long enough to get careless," Queen Abigail spoke up, stroking the soft fur of the little dog that had jumped in her lap to look for comfort.

"Do you know where the estate is?" Alex turned to Celine and Frederich.

"It's North, nowhere near the capital. He had a house in the city he used most of his time in the capital." Although Celine had never visited the estate, she knew Lord Remy possessed vast acreage, not to mention extensive mines in the mountain ranges to the north.

"I wish we had a quick way to get there. Who knows what means he has of sending and receiving messages. If only we still had the mirror." Frederich tapped his fingers together as he thought.

"I think I might have an idea," Celine spoke up, a sly smile crossing her face.

CHAPTER THIRTEEN

"**I** still think you're crazy; I still can't believe it was you in my lodge." Alex turned to Celine, who was riding behind him. It had only taken a few hours for Alex, Celine, Frederich and Lucie to gather a few provisions and mount the sturdiest of King Ruben's horses before heading for the mountains. On the way, Lucie and Frederich had filled him in on Celine's misadventure with Cherry.

"Are you sure you know the way there?" Lucie chewed on her lip as her horse picked its way across a rocky patch of ground.

"I think so." Trying to get her bearings and steer the small group in the right direction, Celine was quickly discovering that the terrain looked distinctively different on the ground than it did from the sky.

"And who's saying they'll even help us when we find them?" Frederich spoke up from his position at the back of the group.

"Of course, they'll help us. I saved their egg; they owe me now." Celine narrowed her eyes, focusing on the trail ahead. Ahead, she spotted a familiar mountain peak. "We just have to get to that mountain." She pointed to the summit.

"Blackdruod Peak," breathed Alex. "Are you sure about this?" He turned questioning eyes to Celine.

"Yes." Celine turned her horse uphill. "It's our only chance."

After an entire day snaking around giant boulders and through towering pine trees, Celine's energy flagged. When they stopped for the night, the mountain towered over them, so high it blocked the setting sun.

Exhausted, the group only took enough time to eat a quick dinner of cold meat and bread before collapsing into their bedrolls. Everyone fell asleep immediately, except Celine, who stared at the fire, sparking from the sap of the pine wood.

"Are you still awake?" Alex whispered from his place nearby.

"I just can't stop thinking about the magic." Celine sat up, hugging her knees to her chest. "I don't understand why it has to cause so much trouble."

"The magic?" Alex asked.

"Yes." Celine fingered a silky strand of hair that spilled over her shoulder. "Everyone seems to either be willing to do anything to get it or is so terrified of it they refuse to have anything to do with it at all."

"Not everyone." Alex looked over at Lucie, who murmured and turned over in her sleep.

"I suppose." Celine studied her sister-in-law thoughtfully. Lucie had only come to terms with her magic after a long struggle and was the first person in Lovan to embrace her abilities.

"There are all kinds of people in this world," Alex continued, turning his attention away from the fire to Celine. "It's like any other quality, who you are inside comes out no matter what kind of ability you have. Lovan needs time—old habits die hard. If you keep doing what you're doing, people will come around."

Celine bit her lip. She didn't like to admit it—even Lord Remy's betrayal shook her to her core.

"You know, we'll always help you however we can. I know my mother can be a bit overbearing," his lips twisted wryly, "but she has a good heart, and she truly cares about the people. And I'll help you if you ever need anything."

Celine nodded, lying back down on her bedroll. Although nothing had changed, Alex's support made her feel better.

The next morning, the horses; breath were frosty puffs of air as they picked their way up the steep slope to the dragon's den. Celine scanned the area for familiar landmarks, but the sparse landscape all looked the same, dull grey rocks looming like jagged teeth reaching for the sky. As they steadily approached the peak, Celine planned what she would say to the dragons when they reached their lair. However, she was saved the bother when, in a rush of hot air and flapping of leathery wings, a dragon swooped down and landed in front of her.

"I thought we left you back at the castle." Hot smoke came out the dragon's mouth as she spoke.

"Hello, Mildred." Celine recognized the raspy voice. She held back, knowing her jittery horse would bolt if she drew any closer.

"Hello, my dear. I see you've brought guests." Mildred eyed the visitors with a disapproving expression.

"Mildred, this is my brother Frederich, my sister-in-law Lucie, and Prince Alex." Celine made the introductions as if she were at a formal tea.

"Lovely to meet you all." Mildred stretched her dragon claws into a clumsy bow.

"Mildred, we were hoping you could help us," Celine spoke quickly. She could see the dragon was getting bored and restless.

"But I did help you. I brought you back to your people." Mildred polished a razor-sharp claw on a sharp rock.

"I know, and I'm more than grateful. But I was hoping you could just do one more teeny, tiny thing. It's about the man who stole your egg." She hoped this fact would be enough to sway the indifferent dragon.

Mildred's head swung up in interest. "Who would that be?" her eyed glittered.

"His name's Lord Remy, one of my father's advisors from the Lovanian court. He hired Karl to take your egg." Mildred huffed a breath of sulfur smoke, causing the horses to start back.

"He's stealing people's power and using for himself. I was hoping you could take us to his estate before he has time to run and escape."

"Just wait until I get my claws in him." The scales on Mildred's back ruffled up. "Wait here, humans; I'll be back in a moment." Mildred sprang up, wheeling in mid-air and heading for the peak.

Less than a few minutes later, she was back, this time accompanied by Hugo. "We left Quinn with the egg. We're not taking any chances leaving it again. Whoever is coming, hop on." She lowered herself, scaly elbows resting on the ground.

The four exchanged glances as they realized that only two of them could go. "You should stay." Celine addressed Frederich and Lucie. "We can't both go, and if something happens, Lovan needs you—the baby needs you. And you too, Frederich. After all, I got us into this mess, I want to be the one who gets us out of it."

"No, I'm coming with you." Alex stepped forward, giving Frederich a challenging look before he could argue more. Lucie stepped forward to give Celine a hug.

"Are you sure?" she whispered. "You know you could let your father take care of this for you."

"Ahem." Mildred coughed politely. "If you're finished with your little discussion over there, we should probably get going."

Celine let go of Lucie, who returned to her spot under Frederich's sheltering arm. Stepping forward, she scrambled up Mildred's side, wincing slightly when her skin scraped against the heat of the rough scales. Alex did the same with Hugo.

"Wait." Lucie ran to Celine, holding out the gleaming sceptre. "Take this. Maybe it can protect you." Celine leaned down over Mildred's side and took the heavy metal in her hand, its weight reminding her of the importance of her undertaking.

With a rush of air, and a flap of her wings, Mildred leapt into the air. They were away.

CHAPTER FOURTEEN

Icy wind whistled through Celine's hair as they sped through the air. The rocky slopes had given way to the deep green of the forest beneath her. Mildred and Hugo had flown high enough to remain unnoticed, and Celine's head spun as she braved another glance at the ground that rushed below her. Hugo and Alex were behind her, and although she didn't dare turn around, she could hear the steady flap of Hugo's wings as he powered through the sky.

"Shouldn't be long now," Mildred called back, her voice cheerful. The deep green trees grew in tidy rows of orchards interspersed with golden fields of wheat. Celine hadn't realized how extensive Lord Remy's holdings really were. He had lived modestly while in the capital, splurging only on the magical items that were in his obsession.

The spires of his castle appeared in the distance. It was on a hill, a small lake lay next to it, with few small boats bobbing in the water.

"Where do you want to get off?" Mildred turned her colossal head as she swept toward the ground, circling the lake. In spite of the vast farmland and well-kept grounds, there were no signs of life— no animals grazing in the pastures, no people working the fields and gardens. An eerie chill trickled down her spine; something about this place felt... wrong.

"Can we land there beside the lake?" Celine was unfamiliar with the layout of Lord Remy's holdings, and she didn't actually have a plan for what was going to happen next, but the back entrance seemed like the best place to start.

Mildred skimmed across the surface of the lake, landing on a smooth green patch of grass near the castle. Celine scrambled down, politely hiding her relief when she felt the solid ground back under her feet. Alex was close behind her, his hair rumpled from the wind.

"Do you think he's actually here?" Alex asked, as he eyed the looming spires of Lord Remy's castle.

"There's only one way to find out." Celine climbed up the hill toward the castle.

The large wooden gate creaked open when Celine gave it a gentle push. They still had yet to encountered anyone. The castle was eerily silent; even the trees were silent, no birds twittered and called from the sky, and no chattering squirrels ran up and down their branches.

Celine stuck her head around the edge of the door to the courtyard. The guardhouse was empty. They slipped through the door, and it banged shut behind them, sending a deafening clang through the silence.

"Where will we look first?" Alex turned to Celine, raising an eyebrow. The castle walls loomed in front of them, full of endless possibilities for places to hide.

"I guess just start at the beginning." Celine strode across the courtyard more, confident than she felt and pulled the handle of what she assumed was the kitchen door. It opened without resistance.

"I guess he doesn't see the need to lock up," Alex commented, a wry expression on his face.

They entered a large entry room, surprisingly clean considering the lack of staff. Celine peered through the gloom, not sure what she was searching for. Ignoring the large staircase spiralling in front of her, she moved toward the back of the hall toward a set of double doors that stood open. Alex followed, letting her lead the way.

Hours later, Celine was ready to give up. They had wandered from room to room, all spotless and decorated with perfect taste and priceless objects. It surprised Celine. She always thought of Lord Remy as being a somewhat frugal and parsimonious man—not at all interested in fripperies. She paused briefly to examine a large painting. A bygone king seated on a throne.

"Alex, look at this." She gestured to the painting. Alex came over, peering at the canvas.

"What is it?"

"It's the sceptre." She pointed to the object in the king's hand.

"Do you know who that is in the painting?" Alex stood close behind Celine, so close her cheek brushed against his tunic, distracting her.

"No, he doesn't look familiar at all." Celine examined the king's face. He had a proud expression, and although his eyes were merely oil on canvas, they seemed to see right through them, making Celine squirm uncomfortably.

"He actually looks a lot like Lord Remy. Just less... chubby." Shrugging, she moved on. The next door was different. Celine knew immediately by the tingle that ran up her hand. She opened it cautiously. It led into a large room that was unlike anything else in the castle.

Celine sneezed; the room was full of dust. Obviously, it had not benefited from the rigorous cleaning that the rest of the castle had enjoyed. Shelves lined the entire room from floor to ceiling, overflowing with strange looking objects.

"This must be his collection." Celine stood in the middle of the room with an awestruck face. She wandered over toward a row of bottles on a shelf. They were clear, about the size of her hand. Inside, the bottle appeared to be some sort of liquid that swirled and turned, almost glowing as it caught the light streaming through the window. Mesmerized, Celine reached to touch one.

"Stop." Alex grabbed her hand, stopping her before she touched the glass. "In case there's anything dangerous, we shouldn't go near anything in this room."

Celine stepped back from the shelves, crossing her arms in front of her chest. "What do you think those are?" her eyes strayed to the gleaming bottles.

"I'm not exactly sure, but there's dark magic at work in here. We have to be very, very careful."

Celine wondered what she was getting into. The sceptre she had tucked into her belt was growing warm, responding to the thick magic that eddied through the room. She touched the sceptre with one finger before jerking it back. It was hot enough to be uncomfortable to the touch.

"Maybe we should go."

Alex nodded in response, and the pair left the room. Celine took a deep breath as soon as she closed the door behind her.

"I've never seen or felt anything like that before." Celine grimaced as they continued down the hall, arriving at a staircase that wound its way up a lofty tower.

"Will we try this? I think we've seen everything on the main floors." Gripping the railing tight as the stairs were steep, Celine ascended. It was dark, with only the light from thin windows cut into the hewn rock lighting the way up the uneven stairs. A small landing, just big enough for two people, was at the top of the stairs. Behind the landing was an ancient looking wooden door.

When Celine grasped the handle, a shock shot through her body, electric in its intensity. "He's in here," she whispered to Alex.

Hoping for an element of surprise, she flung the door open with a shout.

"Hello, my dear." It was Lord Remy, sitting in an overstuffed armchair. In one hand, he held a steaming cup of tea and in the other a plate balancing a large slice of ginger cake.

"Well, don't just stand there; sit down. Have some tea; we can have a little chat." He chided Celine who stood, mouth gaping open, not quite sure what to make of this turn of events.

Numb, Celine moved to a matching chair. It was soft, she thought, rubbing the velvet surface. Her brain felt fuzzy, and she wondered why she was even there.

"Cream and sugar?" Lord Remy lifted his pinky finger as he poured tea into a gold-rimmed cup. He slid a slice of the ginger cake on a plate. "And what about your friend? Will he be staying?" Lord Remy asked in a kind voice.

"Uh, yes, I think so." Celine looked helplessly at Alex. *Why is he here?* she wondered, idly accepting the cup Lord Remy offered her.

"Now. We're all settled." Lord Remy leaned back comfortably in his chair, picking up his plate and taking a bite. He closed his eyes in bliss.

Celine swirled the tea in her cup. She had a vague feeling she shouldn't drink it, but she didn't know why. She set the cup down, hoping she didn't look rude. Lord Remy was such a nice man, it would be awful to offend him. Her sky-blue eyes met his twinkling ones.

"Now, how are you my dear?" Lord Remy pushed up his gold-rimmed spectacles, his face crinkling into smiles.

"I'm well," Celine answered, politely. "How are you?" She racked her brain as her mouth stretched itself into a smile. *There must be a reason to be in this room,* she thought, picking up the tea again.

"And who's your friend?" Lord Remy leaned forward to help himself to another generous slice of cake, scattering crumbs across the silver tray.

"This is Alex." A feeling of surprise nudged Celine. She had completely forgotten about Alex. She wondered absently why he was there with her. Wasn't he supposed to be in Iasia?

"Excellent. I've heard so many things about you and your many.... talents." Lord Remy grinned at Alex, who remained standing stiffly near Celine's chair. "You must give me a demonstration later."

Celine leaned back, looking at Alex. "Talents?"

"Oh, yes." Lord Remy's eyes twinkled cheerfully as he dug his fork into the cake. "Alex has a very unusual gift. I really am quite eager to see it."

Alex pressed his lips together as he took a protective step toward to Celine, standing behind her chair. Celine felt his warm breath stir her hair. He laid a hand on her shoulder. As soon as he touched her, Celine's mind cleared. We're here because Lord Remy is a dangerous man. She shivered as she realized how he had manipulated her. Carefully holding the vapid expression, she formulated a plan. She would have to move fast; Lord Remy was cunning—more cunning than she imagined possible and who knows what kinds of unpleasant things he might have at his disposal.

"You have a magnificent home." Celine had found in the past that flattery was a most useful tool when trying to buy time. "You must tell me all about it. Have you made any changes yourself or has it always been like this?"

"Oh, I've made a few additions here and there," Lord Remy preened, delighted at the chance to show off his accomplishments. "I've had a whole new section added to the garden. Mostly useful plants—for my studies, of course. Althea was invaluable in showing me what to put in it. And I've also added some security features. My predecessors were a bit... lax when it came to safety."

"Of course." Celine nodded wisely. "One must think of safety. And I can't help but notice that you have so many lovely things. Did they come down through the family as well?" Celine knew she was treading on dangerous ground but couldn't help wondering if he was the first to have such an obsession with collecting.

"Oh, yes, my things. Well, most of the paintings and rugs and furniture were here, but I have added quite a few artifacts. Some were very hard to find. I have to admit, I'm quite proud of them."

"As you should be. I would love to see some of them." Celine leaned forward, beaming.

"Certainly." Scraping the last crumbs from his plate, Lord Remy popped them into his mouth and stood up, brushing off his waistcoat. "I'll show you my favourite room of all. I call it my collection room. In fact, I've been thinking there's one more thing I'd like to add to it and need to make some space on one of the shelves. Come, come." He bustled to the door, leaving Celine and Alex to trail behind him.

Celine reached out a hand to Alex. She knew it wasn't appropriate. After all, they weren't engaged anymore, but she needed his touch in order to keep her mind from going foggy again. He wrapped her small hand in his as they followed Lord Remy down the spiralling staircase.

"Are you sure this is a good idea?" Alex whispered. "Who knows what kinds of things he's got stored in there."

"I can't do anything about this unless I have proof of a crime," Celine whispered back. "If I can get him to confess something—anything— in front of us, I'll have more than a good enough reason to fight him. Otherwise, my hands are tied. He's much too popular and powerful in the court; there'd be chaos if we couldn't substantiate ourselves."

"All right, but you'll have to be very careful. We're on his territory and he holds all the cards." Alex gave Celine's hand a squeeze but didn't let go.

As Celine suspected, Lord Remy led them back to the room full of mysterious artifacts. She shuddered in disgust as the thick choking feel of heavy black magic overwhelmed her senses.

"Ah...." Lord Remy rubbed his hands together in glee as he surveyed his ill-gotten treasures. "All my beautiful things."

"You found all these yourself?" Celine stayed away from the shelves so she wouldn't accidentally touch anything.

"Oh yes. I'm afraid my ancestors weren't very open-minded. In fact, until my father passed away, I had to house most of my collection elsewhere. He was very stuffy that way." An unpleasant darkness lurked in Lord Remy's eyes when he spoke of his father. "Very unfortunate that he died so young. A curious expression flitted across his face; so brief that if Celine hadn't been watching him, she would have missed it."

"What are all these things?" Almost against her will, Celine drifted toward the mysterious bottles of swirling liquid.

"Pfft." Lord Remy waved a dismissive hand. "It would take too long to explain every little detail. I'll just show you a few of my favourite artifacts." He headed toward a heavy wooden table in the centre of the room. Celine assumed it was some sort of station for mixing things. Rows of bottles and beakers, some containing strange herbs and substances, filled its length. Lord Remy cleared a space on the table before perusing the bottles, searching for a specific one.

"Here we go." He picked up a bottle identical in size and shape to the ones that Celine had seen on the shelf. He blew the dust off the bottle and gave it a quick wipe with a cloth before sorting through a basket of corks and stoppers, choosing one that fit tightly into the neck of the bottle.

"You see," his voice held a note of pride as he looked fondly at Alex and Celine. "My collection is unlike any other in the kingdom. In any of the kingdoms, really. Where other people have pretty things—although nice, they're not terribly useful—my collection is more... shall we say... sentient." Celine didn't answer, waiting for his ego to fill the silence.

Lord Remy set the bottle gently on the table and went to the shelf. "Do you see this?" He gestured to the bottles, which seemed to glow in the murky light. "These are my life's work. My most prized possession." He touched one reverently with the tip of his finger. "It took me years to learn that all human potential can be extracted and preserved. And then even twice as long to figure out how to do it."

"So—those are?" Celine paused, too horrified by the possibility to continue her sentence.

"Yes. Souls, you would call them. But really, just a collection of memories, abilities, wants, hungers...." He waved a hand. "All ready for me to use. I've searched high and low, and these are the finest in existence— all here for me to access whenever I need them."

"Access?" The word slipped out of Celine's mouth before she could pull it back in. She gazed in dismay at the rows of bottles.

"Oh, yes." Lord Remy pushed up his spectacles, which were sliding down his nose before reaching into his pocket. He pulled out a small golden vial. "I just put a little in here, a tiny pinch, mind you, I wouldn't want to waste it, not after all the effort I've put in. Then, I put it around my neck, so it's touching my skin, and it's as easy as that. I have all the abilities."

"But why?"

"Why? Indeed, why? You don't understand what it's like to be me. Everyone thinking I'm some ignorant backwoods bumpkin just because I'm a little different from them." His voice rose in indignation. "Obviously, you would not understand. You're the precious princess; no one would dare laugh behind your back, ignore you at all the parties, leave you out of their social calendars."

"But you're an important member of the council. Everyone respects you. People love you," Celine protested.

Lord Remy snorted in derision. "I inherited that council position from my father. Yes, people might listen... now. But it took years of work before I even dared open my mouth at a council meeting. All those bloodthirsty warriors just snickered every time I had a suggestion. Fools. They never even noticed when that imposter, the shapeshifter, took your place. I noticed right away. I should have taken her powers—very tempting—but I needed her elsewhere. Besides, she'll come back to me, eventually."

Realising the depths of evil the man had sunk to, Celine couldn't wait to hear more. She gave Alex a meaningful look, hoping he would understand what she intended to do, before putting her hand to the sword hanging from her side.

"I don't think so." Lord Remy smirked as he flicked his index finger. The sword disappeared, reappearing in Lord Remy's hand. "I don't think you'll be needing that where you're going. But first, I need to attend to this friend of yours—an empath, I believe?"

Celine turned to stare at Alex. He gave Celine a sheepish look. "I was going to tell you, but there just wasn't a good time."

Lord Remy hummed. "Very interesting. Well, this has been a lovely chat. It's always so nice to catch up with you, my dear. But I really must get to work now." He turned back to the table, picking up the bottle.

Celine sprang forward and knocked the bottle out of his hand. It splintered to the floor with a crash, sending shards of glass scattering in every direction.

"Alex, get the sword!" she shouted as she brought her knee up into Lord Remy's groin. To her surprise, it was like hitting a solid piece of granite, sending a streak of white-hot pain shooting through her leg.

Lord Remy smiled as, unfazed by her attack, he paged through a heavy book, muttering to himself as he flicked through pages covered with scrawled markings.

Celine looked back at Alex, wondering why he wasn't helping her. To her shock and dismay, he was frozen, arrested in mid-air, an apologetic expression suspended on his handsome face.

Heart pounding against her ribcage, Celine realized she was on her own. She spun, putting all the power she had into a flying kick aimed at Lord Remy's head. Again, she stopped as if she had hit a wall of stone. Crippled by the pain, her mind whirled through her limited options. She had to be quick; Lord Remy was clearly on a mission, and Celine suspected that it had something to do with the fact that Alex was an empath.

A piece of broken glass crunched under her feet, giving her an idea. Maybe she couldn't touch him, but another object could. She scanned the room, searching for something nearby that she could use to test her theory. Edging her way to the table, she fixed her eyes on a mortar and pestle made of heavy granite. She grabbed the pestle and in one motion, flung it at Lord Remy.

Thud. The pestle hit Lord Remy squarely in the forehead, Lord Remy fell to the ground, banging his chin on the table as she went down. He stood up, spectacles askew, rubbing his head with his hand, a spark of anger shooting from his eyes.

So another object could affect him, but not as much as they usually would. Celine had thrown from close quarters, using considerable force; usually, that would have put a man out cold. But she had to keep trying.

Blindly, she grabbed jars off the table, flinging them at Lord Remy, sending showers of broken glass spraying around the room, doing her best to avoid hitting Alex, still frozen in position. Celine was on her own. Despite the force of her attack, Lord Remy still stood, only a few minor scratches to show for all Celine's efforts. To her dismay, the glass was now merely bouncing off him. There must be some other way of stopping him. Celine cast an eye over the shelves, looking for something... anything that she could use.

There, on a bottom shelf, nearly hidden behind a wooden mask, she spotted a copper sword—the same metal as the collar that had contained Cherry. The only problem was that the sword was on the other side of the table, directly behind Lord Remy. Lifting the largest jar over her head in both hands, she heaved it toward Lord Remy. As it slammed down, she launched herself around the table and toward the shelf. Kicking the mask aside with her booted foot, she grabbed the sword, feeling a strange tingle skimming across her body as she clutched it tightly. She whirled, poising to strike.

"No!" Lord Remy's chubby face twisted into an expression of fury and terror.

Celine narrowed her eyes and struck, piercing him in the heart.

Lord Remy fell to the ground, the thud reverberating through the room. Blood pooled under his body mingled with shards of glass. Celine took a step back, nausea bubbling in her stomach. Behind her, she heard breaking glass as one of the tall windows behind her split and shattered into pieces.

"Hello, dear. Is everything all right?" Mildred poked her grey scaly nose in the window. "I sensed magic and not the good kind. Oh dear, it really reeks in here, doesn't it?" She wrinkled her nose and sniffed. "Oh my, I see you've found the copper sword and used it too. Well done, my dear."

Celine never thought she would be as glad to see anyone as she was to see Mildred at that moment. She let the sword slip from her hand, clattering to the floor.

"Is he—is he dead?" She didn't dare look at the enormous figure lying prone on the floor in front of her.

"I'd say he's definitely dead. As a doornail—stop shoving; you can have a look when I'm done." Mildred turned her head and spoke to the scuffling sound beside her.

"Hugo," she tutted, turning back to Celine. "His nose is bothering him as usual. Now, have you finished this business that you came for? I would like to go back and check on my egg."

"I think so." Celine was shaky and disoriented. "Except, for him. He still can't move." A sudden burst of panic lurched in her chest. Alex still wasn't moving. Celine didn't understand why the hold the magic had on him didn't disappear with Lord Remy's demise.

"Oh, yes, I can see what you mean. Well, just use the sceptre to disable it. I know you have it with you."

"I can't—I don't think it works for me," Celine admitted, her face downcast.

"Of course, it will." Mildred's eyes twinkled, "You are the princess, aren't you?"

"Yes. But I don't have any magic to use it with."

"Here, let me show you." Mildred stretched her neck and poked her head inside the room, her fiery breath warming up the chilly air. "All you have to do is clear your mind, then picture what it is you want it to do. The sceptre will do the work for you."

"All right." Celine took the sceptre out of her waistband, letting the heavy metal warm in her hand. She closed her eyes, concentrating on the ridges and patterns of metal, smooth against rough. She thought about Alex, his loyalty, willingness to help her— even when she was a stranger to him. A prickling feeling nudged at her chest and she guided her thoughts and focused them on Alex, willing him to move. She cracked her eyes open.

"Did anything happen?" She looked hopefully at Mildred.

"Not yet. You're too tense. Relax a bit. It's like the sword fighting your so fond of. It takes a little time to get good at it. Just breath in and out slowly before trying this time," Mildred's voice was patient.

Celine took a deep breath and closed her eyes again. This time, she didn't grip the sceptre so tightly. She listened to the sound her breath made, in and out, in and out. Then, she thought again of Alex, thinking of the way his warm brown eyes twinkled when he smiled at her. The way his hand felt when it wrapped around hers. This time, the tingling spark in her chest was a big stronger. She kept her eyes closed. A rustling sound caught her attention.

Celine opened her eyes and looked again; he was moving. Alex blinked and shook his head, staring dumbfounded at the prone figure of Lord Remy in a spreading pool of blood.

"What happened?" his eyes slid to Celine, who was more than a bit dishevelled after her ordeal.

"Lord Remy used his magic on you—he was planning to put you in one of those." Celine gestured to the bottles of swirling liquid on the shelf.

Mildred interrupted them with a shake of her head, reminding Celine of a large dog. "Are we going to go now? It's rancid in here."

"I suppose." Celine looked again at the shelf, reluctance etched on her face. "What should we do with those?" She pointed to the rows of gleaming glass containers. "It would be a shame to leave them here."

"We'll take them with us," Alex decided. "We'll set up a final resting place where people can come and pay their respects."

Mildred and Hugo waited in the garden while Celine and Alex gently placed the bottles in two wooden cases lined with blankets. It was with a great sense of relief that Celine finally climbed out of the window and onto Mildred's back. Flapping her wings, Mildred ascended into the air, circling the castle. Swooping low, she gave a great roar as fire spewed out of her mouth, setting the castle alight.

"That's for stealing my egg," Mildred said with a satisfied air. "Anyway, that place reeked of dark magic; it needed to be gone. I knew you couldn't have anything to do with it, my dear; it would have caused far too much trouble. You humans and your politics." She breathed out another curtain of flames, building up the fire that had already spread to other parts of the building, before diving up into the clear blue sky.

Celine had to admit, she wasn't sorry to see the end of the place where so many dark deeds had taken place. She took a deep breath, letting the fresh air clear her lungs, giving her a sense of lightness she didn't know she was missing. She looked over at Alex, who was balancing on Hugo. He gave her a brilliant smile that sent a fission of excitement running through her veins.

CHAPTER FIFTEEN

Dragons were notorious for avoiding human contact, so when Mildred and Hugo landed on the top tower of the castle, pandemonium ensued. It was only the sight of Alex dismounting that kept a flurry of arrows from being shot at the small group.

Setting her wooden case down carefully, Celine thanked Mildred, even daring to give her a hug, a short one—the scales were hot and prickly. "We never would have survived without you." Emotion filled Celine's voice as she looked into the golden eyes.

"Of course, my dear, as far as humans go, you're not too bad. And that prince of yours is quite nice too. I suggest you keep him." Mildred winked at Celine. "I have a feeling I'll see you again sometime. Maybe I'll even come back for a visit."

"Would you?" Celine bounced on her toes, thinking about the fun they would have when a giant dragon landed at the castle. "You're welcome to come anytime." She gave Mildred another squeeze before the giant beast leapt into the air, circling once then disappearing behind a cloud.

"You're back!" Lucie and Frederich appeared, out of breath from climbing the steps to tower. The next few hours flew by with a flurry of activity. Celine briefed the King and Queen along with Frederich, Lucie and the Iasian council on the actions of the errant lord and their part in defeating him. They decided the three Lovanian royals would leave immediately for Lovan to report to King Erich and Queen

Isabella. At long last, Celine returned to her room, delighted to find Sarah and Louise waiting for her.

"Where did they find you?" she turned to Louise.

"She tied me up and put me in her closet. She caught me looking for the sceptre."

"Where did you get it from, the trunk? I tore her room apart looking for it. Sarah warned me she was planning something really big, and I couldn't sit back and do nothing about it."

Tears came into Celine's eyes at the bravery of her friend. "Thank you for doing that. I'm so sorry that happened to you." She gave the girl a hug.

"Now, it's time for you to get cleaned up... I hate to say it, but you smell just like a dragon." Sarah gave her a little shove toward the large bath that steaming in the corner of the room. The fresh smell of floral soap wafted toward Celine.

"And then," Louise continued, with a hint of cheekiness in her smile. "We're going to make you look more beautiful than you ever have before. After all, you're leaving in the morning and we're going to make sure that a certain prince that will remain nameless won't be able to forget about you."

Louise and Sarah exchanged a meaningful glance.

"I wouldn't be so sure about that," muttered Celine, as she lowered herself into the bath. "He's had plenty of chances, but he has said nothing yet."

"He just wanted to wait for the right time." Sarah reassured her as she added another dollop of scented oil to the water and gave it a stir. "Now, let me wash your hair. Louise will have your dress ready when you get out."

When Celine emerged, wrinkled but refreshed from her bath, she wrapped herself in a fluffy towel. The girls fussed around her, taming the mass of golden hair into smooth ripples that fell down her back. Celine stepped into a gauzy gown, one of Lucie's signature pieces, known for being both beautiful and comfortable. The soft folds skimmed across her silky skin.

"And Lucie sent this for you to wear." Sarah drew a sparkling crown out of a velvet pouch. She pinned it on. Celine tilted her head. The gold metal blended in perfectly with the shining waves of her hair.

"There. Now you're ready." The two girls took a step back, admiring their handiwork.

"It's time for you to go." Sarah pushed Celine toward the door.

The steward led Celine to a place near the head of the table next to her brother and sister-in-law. Queen Abigail had taken it upon herself to send them off in style and had spared no expense. Everything was even grander than usual; the glow of the multitude of candles placed around the room gleamed against the crystal and fine China.

Friendly faces filled the room, many she recognized from her previous visit to Iasia. Now that she had resolved the issue with Cherry, the room seemed lighter, happier. Celine looked up just as Alex entered the room. The last time she had seen him, he was dishevelled and windblown. But now—now he was perfection itself. His jacket and breeches fit perfectly and showed off his dark hair and chiselled features. Their eyes met and for a moment Celine couldn't breathe. She looked away and fidgeted with her fork, hoping the dim lighting would hide the fiery blush on her cheek. He took his place next to her, and a warm tingle enveloped every nerve in her body at his nearness.

"Our last night," he said in a low voice, his smile not quite reaching his eyes.

Celine gave him a faltering smile, wishing she had more time.

King Ruben stood, tapping his spoon against his glass. "This dinner is in honour of our royal guests, Princess Celine, who has so bravely endured the trials and has come out victorious. And of course, the crown Prince Frederich of Lovan and his lovely wife, Princess Lucie."

The crowd toasted the three royals as Celine pasted on a polite smile.

After dinner the musicians arrived, and the dancing began.

"May I?" Prince Alex held out his hand to Celine.

Celine put her hand in his large, warm one and glided to the dance floor. It was an Iasian dance, one that Celine was unfamiliar with, but she soon learned the steps and was laughing as he swung her around the floor. Nearby, she saw Lucie and Frederich also enjoying the moment.

"You're sad," Alex said, searching her face. The music had slowed to a more sedate pace, but Alex showed no sign of wanting to change partners.

"A little," Celine admitted, remembering with an uncomfortable start that Alex was an empath and could sense her feelings.

"Don't worry." Alex chuckled. "I can't read your thoughts, just your feelings. And most of the time, I try to shut out other people's feelings; it's too invasive."

"Is that why you avoid court so much?" Celine asked.

"I suppose. You know, no one's ever asked me that before. I can tune them out most of the time, but it takes a lot of effort. It can get tiring."

Celine breathed a sigh of relief. Some feelings she had around Alex were not something she wanted to share with anyone.... let alone him.

"And, do you tune me out?" Celine knew she shouldn't ask but couldn't resist the impulse.

"Almost always, unless I get distracted."

"Oh." Embarrassment flooded Celine as she wondered what exact feelings had slipped through the walls of his defense.

"I think that's why I avoided you at first." Alex held Celine close as they swayed to the music. "I knew you didn't like what my mother was doing. I didn't want to force you into anything."

"Well, I didn't know you then." Celine raised her lashes, but his face was impassive, revealing nothing.

Before she could say anything else, the music ended. Alex bowed politely and stepped back as his brother, Prince Landry, cut in.

"You've made quite an impression on my brother." Prince Landry—similar to his brother in looks—couldn't be more different in personality. Cheerful and carefree, his smiles were generous and frequent, and he was the last to leave at any social gathering.

"How do you know?" Celine asked.

"Alex is my brother, of course I know. He's been completely different since you showed up, not avoiding court for one thing."

"Really? Did he avoid it that much? What was he going to do when he had to become king?"

"Oh, he planned to join in... eventually. But he worried about so many people depending on him. It weighs on him to have the future of a kingdom resting on his shoulders, especially when he wasn't brought up expecting it to be prince then king."

"I know how that feels." Celine remembered when Prince Frederich had disappeared, and she had to face a future as the queen of Lovan.

"He's gained his confidence since he met you. He saw how you stepped up and took things on, and he realized he can do it too."

Celine's heart warmed to think that she had influenced Alex in some small way.

"He would never admit it out loud, but he's devastated that you're leaving so soon." Landry spun Celine under his arm before swinging her back out again.

Celine worried at her lip as she considered this additional information. She knew if she returned to Lovan without being engaged, her father and mother would waste no time in seeking new alternatives. In fact, Celine suspected that one reason they had held off the search for a marriage partner for her so long was because they hoped the alliance with Iasia would work out.

"Doesn't he know how I feel about him? After all, he has the empath gift."

"He would never use that to invade anyone's privacy, especially not yours. If you want him to know how you feel, you'll have to tell him—with words." The prince smirked at the look of dismay that crossed Celine's face.

"You could go now. He's right over there." Landry pointed out a spot near the refreshment table. As if sensing their attention, Alex glanced up, schooling his expression into his usual poker face.

The music ground to a halt and Celine curtsied to Landry, gathering all her courage to go to Alex. After all, she would leave first thing in the morning. What was there to lose?

Weaving through the merrymakers, she headed straight to the refreshment table to find him. When she finally arrived, after being held back by not one, but three lords, he had left.

Celine scanned the room, forcing herself to remain calm. He had probably gotten caught up in conversation as much as she had. She strolled around the other side of the room, trying to look purposeful enough that no one else would try to stop her.

But he had completely disappeared, lost to the crowd. Celine accepted the hand of the Earl who was claiming the next dance, but even on the floor, she hoped to glimpse him on the dance floor, but she saw no sign of the elusive prince. His usual spot near the king and queen remained empty, and Celine's heart sank as she realized he must have retreated early.

Blinking away the tears that threatened to fall, she forced herself to smile for the rest of the night. She would surely have another chance to see him before she left tomorrow.

THE NEXT MORNING CAME far too soon. After breakfast, Celine dressed in her travelling clothes and made her way to the audience hall where King Ruben and Queen Abigail would issue a formal goodbye to the departing royals.

Well-wishers and curious onlookers packed the hall that morning. Celine surreptitiously looked around, hoping to spot Alex, but he wasn't there.

"Hello, my dear." It was Queen Abigail, resplendent in a brocade gown, jewels glittering at her throat and wrists. "Alex told me to send you his apologies, he's been under the weather since last night."

"I hope it isn't serious?" Celine's heart nearly stopped in disappointment as she realized she had missed her chance to speak to Alex.

"I don't think so. He should make a full recovery soon." Queen Abigail smoothed her hair with her hand, the diamonds winking in the morning sun. "But Landry will be down shortly." She smiled brightly.

After long speeches by King Ruben and several of the council members, they ushered the young royals to the courtyard where crowds of people were waving, all there to see them off. Celine smiled and waved dutifully, covering up the ache in her heart with a beaming smile.

The three royals mounted their horses, opting to ride for the first leg of the journey. The carriages followed behind. Sarah had already seated herself in one of them, with Tommy sitting proudly next to her. He had gotten the official post of looking after Celine's horse when she wasn't riding it and proudly wore the little uniform Sarah had procured for him.

Finally, after much fanfare, they were off. Celine's heart was heavy. A lump sat in her throat as they made their way through streets of cheering people. Alex had never even tried to come and see her off. She waved mechanically to the people thronging the streets. *I must not have meant that much to him after all*, Celine thought, pausing to accept an armful of flowers from a little girl.

The crowds thinned, and the streets crowded with shops and businesses gave way to the rocky terrain that had become so familiar to Celine over the past few weeks.

"Are you all right?" Frederich left Lucie's side to ride next to Celine.

"Never better." Celine pasted a wide smile on her face. "It's such a beautiful day and I can't wait to get home to Mother and Father."

"Well, you got what you came for. The engagement is off, and with no repercussions from the Iasians. I have to say, you've done well there."

Celine's smile slipped. "Oh, yes. Well, I think you underestimated me."

Frederich examined Celine carefully as she put all her effort into looking carefree. Happy.

"Are you sure that's what you wanted? It's all right to change your mind, you know," his voice was gentle.

"I'm delighted that things turned out how they did." Celine's cheeks hurt from smiling.

"Oh well, in that case, we might have a problem. Because someone's coming up behind us, and it looks as if they're on a mission." Frederich shot Celine a grin before resuming his place beside Lucie.

Celine turned in her saddle, craning her neck to see what Frederich meant. Approaching them, in a cloud of dust, was Alex.

"Alex? What are you doing here?" Celine's blue eyes widened in surprise.

"I came to see you." Alex rode up beside Celine, letting his horse catch his breath.

"Oh."

"I couldn't let you leave before telling you how I felt." Ignoring the surrounding people, Alex looked at Celine as if she were the only person who existed.

"How you feel about what?" Celine asked in a low voice.

"You. How I feel about you. When my mother told me we were going to be engaged, I was angry. How dare she take that choice away from me after all my other choices were taken away as well? I wanted so badly to dislike you. But the moment I saw you, I couldn't. It was in the hallway. You had bumped into that serving girl."

"Louise." Celine breathed.

"Yes. And instead of rushing on by like most girls would, you stopped to help her. Even when it made you late. And the more I got to know you, the more I respected and admired you. And eventually that respect turned into more."

"More?" Celine's eyes caught his and held.

"So much more," Alex's voice was a whisper. "I think that you're the sweetest, strongest, most beautiful girl in the world." He reached out and took her small hand in his. His thumb rubbed gently on her wrist as he held it and gradually drew her closer. By now, the others had gone ahead, giving the two a bit of privacy.

"I feel the same way." Celine dropped her eyes, overcome with emotion.

Alex drew her a bit closer and leaned over, pressing his lips gently against hers.

Celine's heart soared. She had, in the past, secretly allowed one or two of the nobles in Lovan to kiss her. She even had a childish fling with an Earl at one point and let him call her his sweetheart for a few weeks—until her father put a stop to it, telling her it wasn't right for someone in her position to be playing favourites. But it had never felt like this. His warm lips moved gently over hers as his other hand moved up to cup her cheek. The horses shifted under them, bringing Celine back to reality with a thump. She glanced at the party ahead, but everyone was keeping their eyes studiously to the front, except Tommy who was bouncing on his knees in the back of the carriage grinning at them.

Celine grinned back as Alex raised their hands, still clasped together in a wave.

"Well, I see you've finally made your move." Frederich appeared beside them. He gave Alex a friendly slap on the back. "Well, what are you waiting for? Let's get a move on." He turned his horse around, kicking up a small cloud of dust.

"Wait, you're coming with us?" Celine noticed the bulging saddlebag strapped to Alex's horse.

"Of course." A wide smile crossed Alex's face. "I couldn't let you escape again, now, could I? Who knows what you'd be up to next, sea monsters, probably."

Celine gave an unladylike snort as she urged her horse back into the formation, Alex riding proudly beside her. "Everyone knows they don't exist."

A FEW DAYS LATER, KING Erich and Queen Abigail received Celine with open arms. An engagement celebration followed, which Alex suffered through. He was becoming accustomed to larger groups of people, he told Celine in private as they walked in the castle gardens one evening.

The council members met the news of Lord Remy's betrayal with sadness; most of them had no idea of his more morbid tendencies. However, a few of them, Lord Gunther in particular, claimed they had been suspicious all along. Lucie was especially disappointed; after all, it was Lord Remy who had stood by her and encouraged her to accept her own powers.

Saddened as she was by all this, Celine found it impossible to stay disheartened for long. Life with Alex was exciting, and she threw herself into planning the imminent move to Iasia.

The wedding was a beautiful day, filled with flowers and all the people Celine loved the most in the world. The next morning, when she woke up, Celine's cheeks still hurt from smiling. But it was her new life she was most looking forward to. Alex and Celine spent a week away in the hunting lodge for their honeymoon. They had such fun that it became their special place, a haven from their busy life at court.

They arrived back from one of such visits one sunny morning. The courtyard was a hive of activity.

"What's going on?" Alex dismounted, stepping around a supply wagon.

"There you are." King Ruben popped his head out of the wagon, beaming. "We're going on a tour of the kingdom. It's about time Celine saw the rest of the country."

To continue the story click the link below to read *TRUE,* **a retelling of Puss in Boots.**

Other Books by Kristina J Jordan

FREE – A FAIRY TALE Retelling of Rapunzel mybook.to/free[1]

Brave – A Fairy Tale Retelling of Beauty and the Beast mybook.to/bravekjj[2]

Strong – A Fairy Tale Retelling of the Princess and the Pea mybook.to/strongkjj[3]

True – A Fairy Tale Retelling of Puss in Boots mybook.to/True[4]

Loyal – A Fairy Tale Retelling of Red Riding Hood

Pretty – A Fairy Tale Retelling of the Princess Frog - *coming in November 2021*

Valor - A Fairy Tale Retelling of Jack and the Beanstalk – *Coming in December 2021*

Thank you so much for reading this book. If you want to hear more about upcoming books **KristinaJJordan.com** and sign up for my newsletter to download your free copy of *Free – the retelling of Rapunzel.*

I love interacting with fantasy and fairytale readers on Facebook, Instagram, and Tiktok. My handle is @kristinajjordanauthor and I'd love to see you there.

---

1. http://mybook.to/free

2.   http://mybook.to/bravekjj

3.   http://mybook.to/strongkjj

4.   http://mybook.to/True

Like all authors, I appreciate honest reviews and love hearing feedback about my books. I'd be delighted if you left an honest review on Amazon Bookbub or Goodreads.

Don't miss out!

Visit the website below and you can sign up to receive emails whenever Kristina J Jordan publishes a new book. There's no charge and no obligation.

https://books2read.com/r/B-A-KPEO-IPHQB

BOOKS 2 READ

Connecting independent readers to independent writers.

Also by Kristina J Jordan

The Crown and the Sceptre
Free A Fairy Tale Retelling of Rapunzel
Strong - A Fairy Tale Retelling of the Princess and the Pea
True A Fairy Tale Retelling of Puss in Boots
Pretty - A fairy Tale Retelling of the Frog Prince
Loyal - A Fairy Tale Retelling of Red Riding Hood